THE
BILLIONAIRE'S
THE INTERN TRILOGY BOOK 1
INTERN

paige press

THE
BILLIONAIRE'S

THE INTERN TRILOGY BOOK 1

INTERN

lia hunt

Paige Press
Leander, TX 78641

Ebook:
ISBN: 978-1-953520-51-7

Print:
ISBN: 978-1-953520-62-3

ABOUT THIS BOOK

The Billionaire's Intern is a classic virgin-meets-billionaire romance - if your idea of classic is scorching hot angst with a plot twist that'll leave you begging for more...

No one's ever called me friendly.

You don't get to where I am by being approachable.

I'm used to seas of people parting for me. Especially in the lobby of the building I own, filled with people who work for me.

Guess no one told the new marketing intern.

She spills her coffee all over me and then offers to replace my custom couture with Kathy Ireland.

Emery is a sweet little blinky-eyed Kansas girl. A kitten in the middle of our shark tank. It's just common decency to protect her. Take her to lunch and get to know her. Wonder why she looks at me like she wants me to eat her alive, but pulls back every time I'm ready to bite.

Okay, so that last one isn't decent at all. In fact, every fantasy I have about her is downright filthy.

Discovering I'm her first?

Well, it gives me even more wicked thoughts about the big... city I can show her.

I've been burned before. Fool me once, right? I built a billion-dollar company by planning for every possibility. Making sure nothing gets past me again.

But I sure didn't see this one coming.

CHAPTER ONE

"I'M TELLING YOU. Now's the time to invest in this. That is, if you're serious."

That line of bullshit is accompanied by a smug look this guy doesn't have the knowledge to back. If there's one thing I hate more than anything, it's being told what to do, especially by someone who doesn't know what he's talking about. And, let's face it, too many people don't.

Still, that fact apparently won't stop the douchebag in the Men's Warehouse suit in my office from trying his hand.

I have to give it to him, though. Most people don't have the balls to challenge the CEO of a business that has hit the Forbes' "must watch" list for the past ten years, not on his own turf, and certainly not in his own office. And they especially don't have the balls to go toe to toe with me in particular. I've got a reputation, I've heard people say. And it's not a nice one.

Sure, the head of that rumor mill is my wife—and anyone who will listen to her. But she would know, wouldn't she? Blythe might be the biggest bitch in the world, but she also knows me better than anyone. Which means if she says I'm a hardheaded ass, I'm definitely a hardheaded ass.

If only I'd known her as well as I thought I did.

Still, Blythe's hardly worth thinking about. I'm not giving her any extra thought, especially not now. Not with business playing out in front of me.

"So, you think this is a sure thing," I say slowly, leaning forward on my desk and knitting my fingers together. "A sure enough thing that I write you a check for one million dollars right now, right here in this office?"

The poor sucker's eyes go wide and he has the gall to look around my office, as if anyone here will help him. Sandy, my assistant, hides her smile by writing notes in her notebook. Ramon, my close friend and business associate, keeps his eyes firmly on his phone. Not even the office carpeting is going to give this sap the time of day. And he can look out the floor-to-ceiling glass window behind me all he wants, too. The city of New York doesn't have any answers, either.

"I tell you what," I say. "I'll sign right here, right now, if you promise to personally pay me back the million if the deal isn't the sure thing you promise. What do you say?"

The already pale guy goes white as a sheet. It's not a good look against his cheap polyester.

"Mr. Duke, you can't be serious—"

"No, *you* can't be serious," I cut in, my voice a warning growl. "You don't come into my office talking about sure things if you can't back your shit up. This meeting is over. Sandy, see him out," I add without an ounce of emotion because I'm already done thinking about this waste of time.

The man barely has time to stammer before Sandy's put a hand on his shoulder to steer him out. He looks ready to melt into the floor, but Sandy gives him a warm smile and a flip of her graying hair and shuffles him out easily. That's why Sandy's a great assistant. Quick, efficient, and the right amount of warmth to balance out the cold that I tend to bring out in people.

"Charming as usual," Ramon says, smirking at me from

his chair. "Why was he here, anyway? You'd never normally let a guy like that in the door."

"Owed his uncle a favor," I say with a shrug. "Whatever. Now he owes me one."

"Want me to do any research into what he was talking about?" Ramon asks.

I glance at Ramon. Ramon's recently been upgraded into the position of my closest friend, and I'm still figuring him out in this new role. We're of a similar age. Both married around the same number of years. The similarities end there. His story went in the direction of a happy wife and three kids and mine, well. Not so much.

Still, no matter what, he's always been a savvy business-man, and if he smells possibility here, maybe I should, too.

"You think there's something to it?" I ask.

He shrugs. "Could be."

I think about it. I've been in the investment business for nearly two decades, and I know it better than I know anyone. I don't want to miss out on an opportunity, but I didn't see anything I liked in Cheap Suit's presentation.

Then again, I have been distracted lately. There's a chance Ramon's caught something I've overlooked.

"Look into it," I say. "But don't let on to the guy. I don't need to waste any more of my time on that douchebag. Come back to me when you've got something solid."

Ramon nods. "You're the boss."

I rub my temples. "Now, to focus on the actual work."

I glance at the file of contracts Sandy dropped off on my desk earlier this morning. There's some wording that I'm still thinking over, a few last concerns. But the guy didn't just bring a cheap suit into my office. He also brought cheap cologne, and it's going to be impossible to think in here.

"I'm going for some air," I say to Ramon. "Get me those numbers by the end of the week, all right?"

Ramon gives me a salute and we both head out, him to his

office and me to the elevators. I'll get a coffee from the café in the lobby or take a walk for a breath of freshly polluted New York City air. As I pass through the pristine office, decked out in the most modern furniture and art available, I can't help but smile to myself. I built this. I took a small company started by my father, and built it into what it is today. Duke Capital shines in gold across the white walls in front of the lobby, a sign of exactly who built this fucking thing. I'm admiring the words, thinking to myself about the contracts, when suddenly, I slam right into something.

No, not something. Someone.

Someone whose perfume smells like rose petals.

Someone soft.

I know the last part because I've caught her hand in mine, but I don't have much time to focus on it because her other hand was holding a tray full of coffees. Key word there being *were* because now, I'm wearing them.

Thankfully, they're lukewarm coffees, but my white shirt's going to be ruined. The suit, too, probably. I'm about ready to let this klutz have a piece of my mind when I rein in my irritation long enough to look at her.

"Oh my God, I'm so sorry!"

Her eyes are wider than any eyes I've ever seen, big and brown, just like Bambi's in the cartoon. She's looking around, trying to figure out what to deal with first, the coffees on my marble floors or the coffee spilled on me.

"I'm so sorry," she repeats, her voice a high, crisp note. "I must not have been looking. I'm so sorry, let me get my handkerchief—"

I can't help it. My lips twitch with an unfamiliar tug. I'm damn near…smiling. A handkerchief? Is she eighty years old?

Of course, she isn't. She's young, with a tight black skirt that perfectly hugs the curve of her ass. Her legs are creamy white and smooth, and as she leans forward to blot my shirt with that damn handkerchief, I get a deep look at the cleavage spilling out of her white bra tucked under her button-down. She doesn't notice me looking, but someone else does. My dick twitches in my pants, alert and ready to respond.

"I can buy you a new one," the mysterious, adorable creature before me says. "I swear. I'll have to wait until my next paycheck, and um…" She stammers here, her eyes flying to mine and then back to the mess on my shirt. "I can pay for the dry cleaning. That's probably less than a new shirt? I don't really know how much men's shirts are, anyway. Oh my God, I think I'm making it worse."

She dabs the handkerchief to her tongue to wet it before going back to the blotting, and yes, she is making *it* worse. Just not in the way she thinks.

I'm entranced, and not just because she's gorgeous. And not because my cock is besotted with her. I've never been offered a reimbursement for anything in my life. Not for a business lunch or for playoff tickets or for the use of my house in the Hamptons. Never. No one offers when you're a billionaire, some unspoken assumption it's unnecessary. Besides I could buy twenty of these shirts and not blink an eye.

Everyone knows that. Everyone, apparently, except Coffee Girl.

Apparently sensing a failed mission, Coffee Girl's big brown eyes fly up to mine apologetically.

"I'm sorry," she says, biting her lip. "I'll make this right."

She turns and scurries to pick up the coffee cups. A secretary rushes over to help her just as my phone buzzes.

Blythe: **Co-eds get you hard in the lobby now?**

God, I hate my wife.

CHAPTER TWO

IT DOESN'T SURPRISE me when I walk back into my office and find my bitch of a wife has beat me there and is sitting in my chair, acting like she owns the place. She leans back, her glossy brown curls tucked back so that I have a clear view of her chest. She knows I'm a tits man and she uses hers to every advantage.

But now? Not even those tits could make me want to spend another minute around the woman. To me, she's a viper, and I don't intend to get bit again.

"She's cute," Blythe says, a smug smirk on her face as she reminds me she's "A little young for you. I didn't know fresh-out-of-college was your type."

I ignore her. Thankfully, the hard-on that hopped up at the sight of Coffee Girl has all but shriveled away at the sight of the ice queen before me. Talk about a boner killer.

"What do you want?" I ask, grabbing the files from earlier off my desk so that she can't look at them. I really need to get Sandy to start guarding this area better from Blythe.

"You know what I want," Blythe says, her voice its usual silky purr. The kind that used to whisper sweet nothings in my ear and ask me to bang her brains out, sometimes on the very desk between us.

I dare to look at Blythe. She's tall and gorgeous, a woman that any man would kill to have on his arm and in his home. Her red power suit fits tight around her every curve, and she's got plenty of them to spare. But once you know Blythe, there's one thing about her that you just can't miss.

The glint in her eye. The one that I used to think was sexy as hell, but that I've now learned is the sign that she's plotting something. Scheming. Figuring out how to hide what she's really planning.

It's hard to believe I ever trusted her or let her in. I didn't recognize her smaller fibs because I was ultimately distracted by the bigger lie. I love you, she'd said. The biggest lie of all.

Blythe's eyes narrow. She knows I'm not going to take her bait, sexy as it might be. She knows I've fizzled on her, and she knows why.

"I'm here for the same reason I was here a week ago, Harrison," she says. "I'm here to get you to sign these damn papers."

She holds up her briefcase, and I know without seeing them that the papers are in there, probably tagged with her obnoxious little sticky notes that say, "Sign here!" As if the reason I'm not signing is because I couldn't figure out where to put pen to paper rather than the fact that I'm guarding what's mine from her. Not to mention, giving into Blythe means losing the leverage I have on her, and with her so deep in my business and my life, I'm not ready to lose that just yet. Not until I'm sure I've turned over every stone of her deception.

And not until I'm done dragging this out for my own entertainment. There are exactly zero reasons to speed this along. Not when dragging it out pisses Blythe off so spectacularly. She's earned it.

"No thanks," I say after a pause just long enough to annoy

her but short enough to ensure she doesn't start speaking again. "I don't think I want to just yet."

"Harrison, you're being an asshole," she says. "We both know you want out of this. Wouldn't you prefer to be out fucking interns or whoever the hell else you want? Just sign and let's get this over with."

I pretend to think about it before shaking my head.

"No, I don't think I will," I say. "See, unlike you, I'm capable of some discretion and self-control. And I'll fuck whoever I want regardless. Signing only gives you things you don't deserve."

Blythe throws up her hands. "You're getting a decent deal, Harrison. I'm just asking for what's rightfully mine."

Instantly, the blood in my body heats up, and not in the good way. What's rightfully hers? What did Blythe ever do in our marriage but take and take and take? Did she work the 60 hours a week it took to build this place from the ground up? No. But she sure as hell found time for—

I'm not thinking about it. I'm not letting her get under my skin again.

"Harrison," Blythe says, once again using my name like a corkscrew digging under my skin. "You can't avoid me forever. I run our charity."

I let out a cold laugh. "You *run* our charity? That's a kind way to put what you do to *my* charity. In fact, it takes an entire team of people to keep you from running it into the ground."

This finally gets Blythe to stand. She might be a manipulative shrew, but she's still proud and stubborn. Most women are.

"I'm doing the best I can," she says. "And Robert says we're seeing tremendous growth."

The words make my insides go cold. She just had to bring him up. I was doing fine ignoring the elephant in the room—

the one she *brought* into the room—but that wasn't good enough, apparently.

Instantly, I'm not seeing Blythe and I fucking on the desk in front of me. I'm seeing her and Robert, a.k.a. my former best friend, fucking on the custom sofa in my goddamn house.

Blythe must think this is just so easy. She can replace one billionaire with his best friend and keep the money from the first guy. She can let that new boyfriend draw on a fundraiser napkin, call it art, and get her to pay $100k, essentially funneling the money right back into her pocket. In other words, she thinks she can continue to mooch off the business that I built, and I'll just roll over and let it happen.

But I won't. Apparently, eight years of marriage didn't teach her that about me. I never close a deal without getting what I want, and I never overpay.

And in this case? I've got all the time in the world to wait her out.

"I'm not signing," I say. "Get out of my chair. Get out of my office."

"No," Blythe says. "Not until you sign these papers."

I smirk at her. "Fine. I'm done for the day anyway."

I grab my coat and tuck the files I grabbed from the desk into my briefcase. I turn, leaving the door open, and catch sight of Sandy hovering nearby.

"Don't ever let her in my office again," I say, loud enough so Blythe can hear behind me.

I hope she hears me. I hope she knows that, this time, her games won't play out the way she thinks they will.

And like hell am I going to lose.

CHAPTER THREE

I SLAM the elevator button once I get to the lobby, closing my eyes for a moment to try to get a handle on myself. Blythe's gotten under my skin, and I hate that she had the power to do that. She knows exactly how to needle me, but she's forgotten that I know her, too. If I want to wrap this up, then there's only one thing to do, and that means a trip down to the sixth floor.

I step into the gilded, mirrored elevator and send it zooming down. As the doors open, I'm in a much more sterile, darker, smaller version of my own floor. Everyone here looks just a little miserable, and maybe I'm kidding myself, but they don't look like that up on Duke Capital.

"Mr. Duke," the assistant at the desk says, her eyebrows rising. "We weren't expecting you."

"I need a moment with Claire," I say. No need to ask if she's available. For me, she has to be. I am her biggest client, after all.

"Of course," the assistant says, standing. "I'll—"

"I know the way," I say, cutting her off.

I head through the office until I get to the back, the biggest office, the one with a view just like mine, albeit a few dozen floors lower. The secretary must have buzzed her because, before I can get there, Claire's already standing to welcome me in.

"Harrison," she says. "What a nice surprise."

"Didn't seem like it to your secretary." I smirk.

Claire waves a hand. "We always have time for you. Come on in."

I walk into her office. It's sparse and neat, which I appreciate. I can't stand a slob. Claire's entire being is neat and clean, right down to her crisp blue skirt and blouse. She gives me the once-over, too, taking in the fit of my suit. Her gaze pauses on the coffee stain, a slight rise to her brow reminding me it's there but she's polite enough not to mention it. Fuck. I'd have changed shirts in my office had Blythe not distracted me.

"I'll make this quick," I say. "I want you to get Blythe off my back."

"Harrison," Claire says, sighing. "The way to get Blythe off your back is to just sign the papers."

I chuckle. "You're so eager to lose me as a client then?"

She laughs, taking a seat at her desk while she looks through the drawers. "Harrison, you've been dragging this out forever at this point. Don't you think you've both suffered enough?"

I might have suffered, but Blythe certainly hasn't. Part of me knows it would be easier to just give in to her, even if it means paying her millions. What's it to me? I can afford it. No, it's the principle of it. It's that Blythe already fucked me over once, and I don't plan to let her do it again.

"I've told you a thousand times, Claire, I don't want her to get a penny," I say.

Claire sighs, running her hand through her long hair. "Harrison, that's just not possible. You didn't get a pre-nup. Now, next time—"

She thinks there'll be a next time? "I don't plan on being a repeat customer."

She rolls her eyes. "I'm just saying that she's owed a certain amount under the law. And it would move this along if you just agreed with what she's asking."

As if she has a right to ask for anything. As if she did anything for this company. I gave her the charity as a pet project, and she's basically run it into the ground.

"We just need to bang this out," Claire says, drawing me back to the conversation. "Get it done with so you can start living your life."

There's a little sparkle in her eyes when she says that. A slight invitation. I'd recognize it in any woman, but especially in Claire. After all, she isn't just an excellent attorney. She's also an excellent fuck buddy, the perfect combination of business and pleasure co-existing. And I can read her tells enough at this point to see the invitation.

Yet…

For some reason, I'm not as hot for her in this moment as I usually am. In fact, I'm a little annoyed—not at her, but at myself. Here's a perfectly available woman, someone's who's a great lay with just the right amount of discretion. But looking at Claire right now, even as she leans over her desk towards me, I feel nothing.

I offer her a grin. "You think I'm having trouble living my life?"

"Of course not," she says, blushing a little. "I just… Don't you want a new life? A *free* life?"

I laugh at her implication. Free to her means the chance to start over with a new someone. It's ridiculous. Of all the people who I thought would understand, it's my divorce attorney. She should know that, no matter what happens post-Blythe for me, there's no great romance hanging around the corner. Not unless you count the one between me and my company.

"Don't worry about me," I say. "Just get Blythe to back off. I don't need her breathing down my neck when I'm working."

Claire holds up her hands. "Fine, Harrison. But if you change your mind…"

I know she's not just talking about the papers, but I don't address it. I just nod.

"Thank you," I say. "I'll be in touch."

After I leave, I head straight downstairs to the sleek black car that's waiting for me. Bless Sandy for having it ready. I slide into the back seat and breathe in the smell of the leather, immediately helping me to calm down.

Action. Air. I'm already feeling better.

"Accident at the office, sir?"

It's my driver, Leo, who says the words. He's an older guy who's worked for me for years, and outside of my own family, there's no one I trust more. He's the kind of guy who knows when to roll up the divider window without a word when he knows there's something about to happen in the back seat that he's not meant to see.

I don't understand his question for a moment until I realize he's talking about the light brown stain on my shirt.

"Oh, right," I say, and then, suddenly, there she is in my mind. Coffee Girl. The total opposite of my ex-wife. Adorable, sure, but also hot. I imagine her biting her lip as she blotted my shirt with her handkerchief. That girl couldn't lie if it was her job. Not like Blythe. So young, so innocent, and so not anyone I need to be thinking about.

Just the memory of her makes my cock twitch in my pants. It's not a memory I want to relive in front of Leo, though.

"Just a little spill," I say.

Still, the memory's jolted something in me, something that was conspicuously absent when I was in the office with Claire. Why is some split-second encounter with a random new hire enough to light a fire for me, but Claire practically throwing herself across the desk wasn't doing it?

I shake the thought off. Clearly, I've just gotten bored of Claire. There's also the complications with the divorce. Too much Blythe tied into that relationship. That's got to be it. It doesn't surprise me. Basically anything Blythe ever touched is a turn-off for me now, so it doesn't surprise me that Claire's lost in that, too.

Leo weaves through the traffic, and soon enough, we're at my place on Park Avenue. It's one of my favorite places in the city, a building that bridges modern convenience with timeless charm. From the wall-to-wall marble in the bathrooms to the fumed oak flooring throughout the rest of the place, everything about it screams the height of luxury. Essentially, only the richest and wealthiest make their home here.

In other words, people like me.

I head up to the eleventh floor—my apartment spans both the tenth and the eleventh—and toss my briefcase on the table. It looks like Gladys was already here to clean today, and the whole place smells like rich pine cleaner. I pour myself some bourbon and settle into the leather couch in the living room. Even though my briefcase will need to be dealt with eventually, I've got other things on my mind. Things I need to beat out. Literally.

My hand goes to my belt. I can already feel my hard-on throbbing before I manage to unzip and get a hand around myself, shutting my eyes, head dropped onto the back of the sofa. Normally, at this stage, it's a faceless woman that I jack off to, just a pair of tits that bounce in front of me. But now, there's someone else in my mind. She takes me off guard.

Coffee Girl, surfacing again after my thoughts in the car. I imagine it's her waiting for me in my office instead of Blythe. She's in one of my white button-down shirts, unbuttoning it as I walk in. Her tits are heavy and supple, her nipples sharp points under the thin fabric. She smiles at me and bites her lip. The wicked desire inside me spikes, hot and ready.

"I think I need to be punished for what I did to your shirt," she says, her voice a delicate whisper.

I close the distance between us in a few steps and rip the shirt off of her, buttons flying to the sides of the room. I don't care that the door's still open behind me and anyone could come in. Fantasies needn't be troubled by pesky realities.

Coffee Girl wraps her legs around me and grinds against my hardness, whispering how much she wants me to fuck her right here, right now. In the fantasy, she's soft and sweet, her kisses desperate and pulsing with need. She's wet and slick and when I plunge into her, her gasp is endless and perfect.

I work my hand harder and faster against my cock as in my mind, she emboldens me with filthy whispers and whimpers of encouragement. I'm pushing myself to the edge, working the inflamed flesh until I'm fit to burst, and then I come into my hand, spilling out as I shudder.

The episode leaves me breathless for a second with Coffee Girl still hanging over me in my mind. I don't want to be here, beating off to a fantasy of her. I want her here. I want to show her everything a man of my experience can do to a woman like her, how I can make her cry out my name again and again and again.

But Coffee Girl's still young. She's probably got some boyfriend here that she thinks she's in love with. Or maybe he's still back home. I got a midwestern vibe from the girl, and that's it, she's probably pining for some farm boy that's never fucked her any other way than missionary or bent over a hay bale. For fuck's sake.

Oh, the things I could show her. But then, a girl like that probably wouldn't touch a guy until he'd dropped the l-word. And that's one thing I'm definitely done with for good.

Leave love and romance to the tourists like Coffee Girl. I'll keep my realism and my sanity.

CHAPTER FOUR

THANKS TO LAST NIGHT, and a healthy run on the treadmill this morning, I've driven all thoughts of a certain wife out of my mind, and I'm ready for the day of meetings ahead of me. It helps that they're meetings I'm actually excited about. Some CEOs might see them as mindless or a waste of time, but every part of my business thrills me. After all, I've built every single thing around me. I control every cog in every machine in this building. And I did it by myself.

Dad was always big on doing things by hand. He'd tell me that a man doesn't really own something unless he knows how every part of it works. When I got my first car—a shitty old Toyota Camry—he forced me to learn about every part on that car. He'd quiz me on how I could fix different things if they broke. He never even let me drive it until I could prove that I could change a tire, replace a brake pad, and swap out the battery.

Eventually, I knew the car like the back of my hand. And I've applied the same approach to the business. I know every inch of the development process, and no matter how many times Ramon reminds me that I'm the CEO and I don't need to be doing it anymore, I never stop looking for investment opportunities. Every new start-up is a chance for another million. Every small yet surprisingly hip restaurant could be hiding the next worthy chain that'll line my pockets. It's part of the hunt for me. I never want to miss something, especially something that's been overlooked by another company.

I found one of the people we're meeting with today. A girl who thinks she's got the next hot streaming service, even though it feels like everyone's already cornered the market on it. But she claims she's landed on something no one else has, a completely untapped market. I got the tip on it from a friend of a friend, someone who told me none of the big shots are taking her seriously. They're letting misogyny get in the way, apparently, or so my friend says. There's some high risk involved. And, though my friend wouldn't get explicit about it, something risqué in addition to risky.

Sandy's arranged the other execs in the conference room; my usual place at the head of the table's empty. I enter last, and conversation stalls to a hush as everyone falls over themselves to wish me a good morning. It's a good team that I've assembled, a mix of perspectives. I know a true business mogul doesn't just hire yes men. He turns people into yes men because he does his damn job.

"Hey boss," Ramon says, nodding at me as I slide into my chair. "How you doing? Heard yesterday ended in some fireworks."

My eyes cut to Ramon. This is one of his biggest flaws. This is the kind of shit you're not supposed to say out loud. And even though he wasn't exactly shouting right now, he should know better. I force a neutral expression on my face.

"You're misinformed," I say, voice cold. "I left early to get some fresh perspective on some contracts."

"Oh," Ramon says, clearly realizing he overstepped and retreating into his chair. "Sorry. I didn't mean anything by it."

All around me, people stare at their notes and click their pens. I realize I've been too harsh. The guy's just trying to be my friend. I'm so used to vipers that I've gotten used to lashing out for nothing.

"Everything's fine," I say, softening my tone a little. "Are we good to go for today?"

He nods. "Just waiting for Sandy to bring the guest. Should be any minute now."

"I think they're on their way," I say, nodding to the glass that separates the conference room from the rest of the office.

I watch Sandy approach with the guest. She looks like an LA type, but not the blonde-bimbo variety. She's got short, dyed black hair and lots of eyeliner. Tattoos are visible on her arms and a few on her ankles. Alternative but grown-up in her suit jacket, skirt, and heels.

"Good afternoon," she says in a husky sort of voice. "It's a pleasure to be presenting to you all. I'm Monica Ortiz, and I'm very excited to be getting this opportunity to present to Duke Capital."

"And I'm wondering how you got such an opportunity," Nathan, one of my younger executives, says, not bothering to lower his voice. He's one of those who's still learning that just because he has some business knowledge doesn't mean he's the smartest guy in the room. There's an awkward chuckle around the table.

I flash Nathan a look. "And I'd remind you, Nathan, that I handpicked Monica to present. You'd do well to treat her with more respect."

Nathan looks around the table for someone who agrees with his take, but no one does. Ramon, in particular, glares at him until Nathan's thoroughly cowed. Standing at the front, Monica gives Nathan a smile that I'm thinking he definitely doesn't deserve.

"Believe me, I understand how valuable this opportunity is," Monica says. "Which is why I don't want to waste a minute of your time."

The other executives exchange pleasant nods and smiles. They like her humility, and so do I.

"The opportunity I'm presenting today is a unique one," Monica says. "A chance to carve out a space that's guaranteed to always have a customer."

She smiles around at the table before passing out a printed brochure. I let my gaze sweep the room to watch the reactions. I've told them nothing about the presentation outside of it being a streaming service and a Los Angeles executive.

"As a woman, it's difficult to find a streaming service that caters specifically to your needs—specifically, a woman's sexual desires," she says. "Movies on services like Hulu or Netflix are too safe, too soft. But head over to services like Pornhub and all you'll find are movies that are made from the male lens, the male perspective. I want to offer something different. A service built by women, for women. Something that delivers on their every fantasy, with new, original content added every month. That's what Pink is."

I was right to watch my fellow executives. Many of them let out uncomfortable laughs or stir in their chairs. One of my female executives, Patti, sits up in her chair. A secret deviant? Perhaps.

"People get bored of the content on streaming services," Monica continues. "There're only so many times you can rewatch *New Girl*, after all. But people will never get bored of porn. Porn will always be there because *desire* will always be there."

Behind Monica, the conference door swings open and closed as someone enters, their high heels clicking on the words *desire will always be there*. I'm not looking over yet, still watching my executives attempt to formulate their thoughts, so I don't focus on the newest member of the conversation until she's walking straight toward me.

Until I notice those magnificent tits spilling out just a bit over the V-neck of her tight black sweater.

Coffee Girl.

True to her nickname, she's carrying a tray of coffees that she gingerly sets in front of each executive as she checks a scrap of paper that's clearly got all of our information written on it. She's diligent. Detail-oriented. And making my cock harden as I watch her pivot in those little kitten heels.

"It's an interesting idea, Monica," Nathan says, his voice dripping with his signature patronizing tone. "But I don't think it's appropriate for us. We've got a reputation, an image. Something like porn feels slimy."

"I'm not sure it's cohesive with our portfolio," Tom, another executive, agrees.

"Why?" Patti snaps back. "Because it's sex-positive? Because it's woman-led? Tell me. What part of that wouldn't be 'cohesive' with the portfolio?"

Tom blushes. I smirk. I glance at Coffee Girl to see if she's paying even the slightest bit of attention, but she just keeps on with her notes and her coffee and her bending over.

"Let's be honest," Nathan says. "This is a man's company. We own a fucking hockey team for crying out loud. We buy businesses that have broad appeal. This is limited."

"I'm sorry, are women not part of broad appeal?" Carrie, another female executive snaps. "I think this would be great for us. And if we get the marketing right, we could make it something really slick. After all, what sells better than sex?"

"We'll be boycotted," Nathan says. "The prudes will come out in full force."

"They boycott no matter what," Ramon argues, clearly won over. "When we contributed to the launch of that new documentary production company, remember? We got death threats from all sides of the aisle."

I listen as they ping-pong back and forth, absorbing their dialogue. Monica stands there, probably used to this by now, her life's work being dissected by a bunch of assholes with wallets. The whole time, though, all I can think about is

Coffee Girl moving closer and closer to me. I see her legs wrapped around my waist in my fantasy, her smooth skin brushing against mine. The way her pussy would clamp around my cock, her lips against my ear, demanding I go deeper and deeper inside her.

Suddenly, she blinks and looks up at me, her big doe eyes going wide as if she saw my thoughts. There's a spark that ripples between us as her mouth falls open, the word *you* on her lips.

Me, I think.

"Coffee Girl," I say suddenly. "Do you like this?"

She stares at me, eyes jolting from me to Monica to the executives at the table.

"Pardon me?"

God, her little voice. I want it to be moaning my name.

"Do you like this pitch?"

"I—I didn't really hear it."

I nod at Monica. "Monica, would you mind going through it once more?"

She looks surprised but only for a moment. Soon, she's launched back into her pitch, careful to thread in small answers to the concerns brought up by my executives. I smile. She's good.

"And that's it," Monica says. "A woman-owned, woman-driven porn service. And in our modern times, you'll never find a product like this that's only guaranteed to grow."

I nod and turn to Coffee Girl, waiting for her response. Her blush as she digests this information only makes my cock twitch more.

"Well," she says. "It's, um, I can see how it might be risky. Might alienate some people. But I think the reality is that there are a lot of women out there who could use this. It's a safe way to figure out what you like, right? And to test out, uh, fantasies. To figure out who—I mean, *what*—you want."

She meets my eyes on those last words. She tugs a little on

her sweater, a nervous habit, probably, exposing just a hint more of cleavage.

I think about this. Then, with a nod to Monica, I say, "Thank you for your time, Ms. Ortiz. We'll be in touch. The rest of you, I'd like the room."

Everyone nods. It's not unusual for them to be dismissed. They grab their papers, their briefcases, their coffee cups, and start to stand. Coffee Girl visibly exhales in relief as she turns to head for the exit.

"Not you," I say, interrupting her retreat. "You stay."

CHAPTER FIVE

"SO," I say, once the room empties except for her. "Do you really believe what you said there? You think there's a space here for Pink?"

Coffee Girl's eyes narrow and she puts her hands on her hips. "I wouldn't have said it if I didn't believe it."

I arch an eyebrow. "Really? And where'd you learn anything about investments?"

I don't mean it as a dig, but she clearly takes it as one. Her lips form a little pout that I can't help picturing a little closer and little lower to me. How it'd feel to have those perfect little pink lips around the head of my cock.

"I make a point of learning about the businesses I work for," she says. "I believe it's important to know their standards."

My lip quirks. "And you think porn meets our standards?"

She blushes, flustered. "I already said what I think. And I stand by it. Is there anything else you need from me?"

I smirk. Yes, there are lots of things I *want* from her. Need's another story.

Still, I like that she spoke her mind. More than that, I'm

surprised that she's in favor of something so erotic. She said she could see young women working out their fantasies through it. The thought sends a naughty picture straight to my mind, one of Coffee Girl splayed out on her bed, her fingers grazing the folds of her pussy, testing and teasing the flesh as she imagines her own fantasies. What are they, I wonder?

"So," she says, yanking me back to reality. I wonder if she can see the lust in my eyes. I'm not bothering to hide it. I probably should. There's an innocence with her that can't be denied. But at the same time, a girl who could say what she just said...can't be *that* innocent.

"I just was wondering," she says, glancing at the floor and back up again, "I mean, did the stain come out? Is that why you wanted to talk to me? To collect your reimbursement?"

For a second, I have no idea what she's talking about. And then I remember. The coffee spill. The suit. She actually thinks I intend to make her pay for it. More than that, she thinks I *want* her to pay for it.

"Do I strike you as the type to scrub out a shirt in the executive washroom? Either it comes back from the cleaners stain-free or it doesn't come back."

"Oh," she says, blushing all over again. I wonder if she goes that pink all over. I wonder if she tastes as sweet as she looks.

She bites her lip again. "I guess I just forget that some people..."

"Aren't on a budget?" I say with a laugh. "Thanks for confirming for me that we aren't overpaying the interns, by the way."

Her eyes narrow. Annoyed. Maybe I'm being too much of a dick. She must be nervous about upsetting me, the boss.

"I was just trying to be conscientious," she says. "I didn't want you to take me for one of these people who think you're just made of money. I have more respect for you than that, Mr. Duke."

She does, does she? And how much does she know about me?

"What's your name?" I ask.

"Emery," she says. "Emery Mills."

"And what do you do for me, Ms. Mills? You're new, I assume?"

It's odd that I don't know. I don't remember hiring her, though, obviously, I trust someone else with that process. But I usually make a point of at least glancing at the applications. It's part of my knowing everything business. And I feel like I would've remembered hiring a girl like this. Her wide-eyed face. Her long hair pulled back into a high ponytail. The kind of body I'd like to bend over and make shudder against me.

"Yes, I'm an intern," she says, looking at me curiously. "I'm just helping out a little everywhere until they figure out a place to put me."

Realistically, I know I'm a pervert for reading into every innocent word she says, but my cock has already thought of half a dozen places to put her since she uttered the sentence.

"Really," I say, clearing my throat. "And what are you liking the most so far?"

I can't lie. I'm hoping she'll say me, the boss. One of her eyebrows rise.

"So far, it's been mostly coffee and copies," she says. "But I like it. Just being here... There's so much activity. So many things are happening. So much energy." She brightens, waving her hands a bit before elaborating further. "I meet new people every day. In the copy room. In the elevator. Waiting in line for fancy coffees. It's really exciting."

Is she seriously glamourizing office life? I love what I've built at Duke Capital, but even I wouldn't be waxing poetic about our copy machine.

"You seem pretty easy to impress," I say. "If only our clients were so easily won over."

She tilts her head, that ponytail swaying, brushing the skin of her neck. I imagine biting it.

"I actually have incredibly high standards," she says. "Both for myself and those I choose to surround myself with."

Does she now? And how do I rank on those high standards so far?

"Then I'll expect a full and detailed report," I say, standing and daring to step closer to her. "I want to know that this is a well-oiled machine, Ms. Mills. If you find that anything's not operating at the level it should be, I hope you'll let me know."

I keep a smirk on my face as I look down at her, taking in all of her features, from those long lashes to her button nose to her perfect lips, currently in a small "o" shape as she stares back up at me.

"Of—of course," she murmurs. "I—"

Her stomach rumbles, cutting her off. Her eyes widen again, clearly embarrassed. She steps back, the brief spell between us broken.

"Have you had lunch?" I ask, surprising myself with the question. I don't know why I'm inquiring. Am I...inviting her? What the fuck am I doing?

Coffee Girl must be thinking the same thing, though I don't know why *she*'s surprised. She's gorgeous. She must be invited to lunch all the time.

By guys in the copy room.

But CEOs engage with interns, don't they? I've definitely called an intern into my office before to pick their brain on something. I must have. Maybe.

"I have to work," she says, glancing around. She knows just like I do that there are eyes watching us right now through the glass walls.

"I own the company," I remind her. "You work at my pleasure."

At the word *pleasure*, I watch a little shudder go through her. She sucks her bottom lip into her mouth and her eyes drop ever so briefly to the floor, or my pants. Hard to tell.

There's a saying about never mixing business with pleasure. Fuck it.

CHAPTER SIX

"NEW YORK JUST..." she trails off with stars in her eyes, a wistful little sigh followed by a playful roll of her eyes. I'm not sure if she's amused or embarrassed by her own excitement. "Captivated me," she continues. "My very first visit, back in high school and I was hooked. One trip and I knew my future was here. I knew I wanted to be here. *Had* to be here."

It didn't actually take much convincing to get Emery to go to lunch with me. Not that she could have easily refused, after my reminder that I'm the boss. I suppose that was a dick move to use to my advantage, but it's just lunch. "Let's go," I'd said and she'd paused for a brief moment, eyeing me before shrugging in agreement, the hint of a blush covering her cheeks before she'd averted her eyes.

Outside on the sidewalk she stood out like a bright light. Not just because she'd slipped into a light pink coat when the New York uniform is a never-ending shade of black, but because her face lit up, her eyes widening in delight at the everyday, normal hustle and bustle of a New York sidewalk.

"I'm still taking it all in," she tells me now from her seat beside me in the back of my car, Leo at the wheel. "It's just so different from everything I've ever known. Kansas doesn't have anything like this."

She gestures to the people hurrying past and to the skyscrapers that soar over us. The way she looks at it all, it might as well be a fairy tale. She's completely lost in the city's magic. Magic that, I'll admit, stopped being real for me a long time ago, if it ever was. Did I ever look at New York with this level of hope and optimism?

Doubtful.

Entitlement and ambition, more likely.

Which is what you need to survive in a city like this. A city that, when you scrape the frosting off on top, is not a fairy tale. It's cold and hard, ready to stab you in the back and steal your wallet at the same time. Only the hardened survive.

In other words, Emery Mills is in for a rude awakening unless she gets her tight ass back to Kansas soon.

Kansas. Ha. I had her number all right. Farm girl through and through.

"Did you grow up here?" Emery asks me, turning briefly from the window to look at me.

"Yep," I say. I avoid mentioning that in reality it's not quite the theme park she imagines. "I decided I'd see my name across one of those skyscrapers one day. And then, I did it."

She shifts in her seat to really look at me, and as she does, her skirt hikes up just a little higher, exposing a creamy thigh.

"You make it sound so easy," she says. "Just make a decision and 'poof,' there it is. The dream."

I laugh. A real one. "Like hell I did. Everything I did, I built from scratch. I started with a few thousand dollars that I got from a job selling Christmas trees. I heard a guy selling a good idea with no one to pay him for it, and I realized, I could do that. I could be the guy with the money."

"But you had no money?" Emery says, a little giggle on her gorgeous lips.

"Not enough," I say, which is true. "But I knew how to persuade people. I'd watched my dad run his business for years, and I learned from him. So, one deal after another, I made it. I learned every piece of the industry. I bought things other people wouldn't touch."

"You took risks," Emery says, impressed.

"Calculated risks," I correct. "It's a necessity in this business."

I realize I like telling her my story. So many people feel like they know me because they can pull up a Wikipedia article. But a paragraph on the web doesn't cover much of what makes a person tick. It's mostly dry facts. My ranking on Forbes, my articles in *Billionaire* magazine. Quotes about money that I made during some interview. Analysis from people who think I should or shouldn't have bought something.

No one who actually wants to know anything about me. They just want to know what I know about making money. My secrets to success. Of course, they never want to hear me say it took a lot of damn hard work and sleepless nights. They just want to skip to the cars and the penthouses and the famous models.

As if it's that easy.

"We're here, sir," calls Leo from the front seat. I've asked him to take us to one of my favorite lunch spots in the city, an Italian place called Charlie Bird. The sidewalk is on my side so I slide out of the car first and give a hand to assist Emery to the sidewalk.

She looks at me, thoroughly bemused.

"I take it your Kansas boyfriend wasn't a fan of chivalry?" I ask and the words are out of my mouth before I realize I'm digging for information.

She purses her lips. "I never mentioned a Kansas boyfriend, Mr. Duke."

"Good," I say. "Then you moved to New York alone?"

"That's very forward of you," she says. "Should I be asking about your wife?"

The question strikes a hot bolt of disgust through my body. I'd managed to forget the existence of Blythe for most of the day and she's the last thing I want to think about now.

Emery's picked up on my mood. She raises an eyebrow, a question. Of course she knows that I'm married. Technically. Legally, whatever. Everyone does. I assume it's also well-known it's not going well. That it's over, save for the ink. It's not exactly a secret. But this girl, this young woman, has seen my wife—God, I hate that word—in my office. She probably doesn't know what to make of what she's heard, and I certainly don't plan on giving her more information than she needs.

"It's complicated," I dismiss, as if it's that easy.

She opens her mouth to protest, but I head forward to the maître d'. They've already got my private table in the upstairs area for me. It's got a great view of the city, and I realize how much I'm looking forward to seeing Emery's reaction. If the sidewalk in front of Duke Capital impressed her, she'll be positively glowing in a moment.

As I expected, her eyes sweep over the room with complete awe. She gives everything in the room this look, from the wooden floors to the hanging chandeliers. Easy enough to impress, I think, and then I remind myself it's because she's so young and inexperienced. When you haven't seen much of the world, it all seems remarkable.

"This is to die for," Emery says when the bread arrives, practically moaning at the carbs. "How do you not just come here and eat the free bread?" She hums in pleasure then pauses, a frown making her scrunch up her nose. "Wait, is the bread complimentary? It should be because we didn't ask for it but you never know in New York, you know?"

I laugh. Fuck me, she's earnest. Wholeheartedly earnest over the city and carbohydrates and God knows what else, but I'm sure there's a long list of things Emery finds joyful. Blythe rarely enjoyed bread, or food, generally. In fact, she was more concerned with who saw us at a restaurant than the restaurant itself. In that way, Blythe's her opposite once again. Blythe was never impressed by anything.

"I didn't mean to bring up a sore spot," Emery says, deftly redirecting the conversation back to where she wanted it. "Your wife, I mean."

Was my disgust that hard to read? "As I said, it's complicated."

Emery nods, seemingly weighing out something before she speaks.

"You know, my parents were divorced," she says, and I stare at her, both impressed and annoyed by her ability to press me. "It was hard to watch. I can't imagine what it's like to live it."

No, she can't. This girl from the farm with her New York dreams doesn't yet know what it's like to have her heart ripped out. She hasn't experienced betrayal in the worst way possible. In a way that eats at the very fiber of your being. I hope it stays that way.

It surprises me to think that. Not that I want her to live like me, but because there's something so pure about her. I want her to believe in those silly dreams.

"We're separated currently," I say, offering her crumbs, my gaze flickering from her rapt attention to the view and back. "It's been contentious and, as of now, there's no end in sight."

Emery nods. She takes a bite of bread, chewing it gingerly.

"And," I add, "we no longer live together."

I have no idea why it feels like important information for her to have, but it does. I don't want her thinking that I'm still sharing a bed with that shrew. As if I could after what she's done.

I think Emery wants to ask more questions, but I won't be answering them. She's an employee, an intern, and she doesn't need to know what Blythe's done. The shame's too much for me even now. The memory of walking in on it is still far more vivid in my memory than I care for.

"What about you?" I ask, changing the subject before she can continue to pry. "Where do you live?"

"East Harlem," she says. "With my roommates."

I laugh. I can't help it. "Jesus, East Harlem's a shithole."

She smiles. "Oh, not at all. We've made it really cozy. And I get to live by the park."

I feel like that's pushing it a bit, but she's so damned awestruck that I don't have the heart to correct her.

We finish our meals, the conversation easy with Emery offering up more odds and ends about her life. She tells me about a sister who's finishing up a law degree and about her family dog, Sherman, who's relatively famous on Instagram. It's the kind of shit I normally would never ask about. It's the kind of shit I normally would not care about. In fact, if it were any other woman, the only interest I'd have in that mouth is it wrapped around my dick.

Instead, I find that I'm actually, shockingly interested. We get back in the car with Leo, and the entire time I keep asking myself why. She's an intern. An employee. Young. Yet, distractingly sexy. Provocative as fuck, without trying. But still, not my type.

Keep it friendly, asshole, I mentally lecture myself. She's likely half my age. She works for me. Worse, she's filled with optimism. Like a little ray of sunshine.

It would be best for everyone to keep this professional.

Besides, her blushing and my ego aside, it's not likely I'm her type any more than she's mine. I'd be a better fit for her if I was a broke artist or bartender. Or...nice.

I should call Claire.

That's decided.

But then, Emery catches sight of a dog walker through the car window. A dog walker walking an entire pack of dogs at the same time. Six, eight. I don't know. I don't care. It's not unusual in New York. But Emery lights up at the sight, tapping my thigh with one hand to get my attention while pointing out the window with the other. Because she's delighted and it's her nature to share whatever she's delighted by. And—

Fuck.

CHAPTER SEVEN

I SPENT last night fighting off thoughts of Emery. Our lunch stuck with me the rest of the day, which I hate. I hate the distraction. I hate the…weakness. For a woman I haven't so much as kissed. I kept picturing her smile and the way she leaned forward as I talked about my background. I thought over what I'd shared and wondered why I'd even given her those details, no matter how small they were. Hell, why had I invited her to lunch in the first place?

There's something else at work here. If this were another time, I could've asked Robert what he thought. He was one of the only friends I would've trusted with such sensitive information. But since he wasn't here—because, I reminded myself with a jolt of cold reality, he was fucking my wife—I was forced to interrogate myself.

Which I despised.

I'm still thinking about it this morning as I shave, running the sharp razor over my jaw and down my neck. The reality is that I'm a man with everything. The CEO of my own company. A visionary. A man who doesn't want for a lay. I've got any number of women in my phone who I could call up and have here, moaning on my bed, within thirty minutes.

Maybe that's the problem? There's no challenge to those women. I know they'd beg if I asked. I know they'd moan in pleasure without asking. With Emery, I don't know. I think she's attracted to me. The blushing, the lip biting, the flare of arousal in her gaze. That was all real, right? I saw it. The way her eyes lingered on me and her skin flushed. But. There's always the possibility she's not interested. Maybe she's just shy or intimidated or enjoys practicing at flirtation.

Then there's the fact that I shouldn't be pursuing her at all. She's young, practically a child in the ways of the world. A girl who's never had her heart broken, or if she has, it was a simple break, the kind that ends in a goodbye kiss and some leftover memories to be reheated on a lonely night. Nothing real or devastating.

I need to put her aside, I decide. Bracing my hands on the sink I examine myself in the mirror for this mental tough talk. Emery deserves to live in her safe bubble, believing the lies of romance and love, for a while. I won't think about her. Won't pursue her. Besides, I have bigger things to worry about. More contracts and, always, the next big idea, looming in the distance. There's the possibility of Pink really being a gold mine. I need to make decisions to keep my business booming. Pussy can't be what distracts me, no matter how appealing it might be.

Exhaling I stand straight and finish up the shave before dressing for the day. Once I'm in the car with Leo, I scroll through my phone, glancing at the stock market and flipping through my email for any particular fires. It's all boring, run-of-the-mill stuff, though there is the daily email from Blythe asking me to sign the papers. She claims she's giving me a final chance to do this right. *Fuck her*, I think, as I delete the email.

Ramon's in the lobby, waiting for an elevator, when I walk in. He gives me a wave, and I fight the annoyance that's started to bubble up for me whenever Ramon's around. It's not Ramon's fault that he managed to marry a nice girl and have his nice family. I can't keep holding that against him. *He's a good guy*, I tell myself. Besides, he's the best I've got. Shockingly, no one else lined up for that vacated best friend role.

"I've been putting out those feelers I promised," he tells me. "And I think our instinct was right. There's something to the idea the kid pitched. I'm not totally convinced, but I'm getting closer. I'm having drinks with a friend of mine to get more intel."

"Yeah?" I ask, feeling a little guilty that I'd forgotten about it. "It felt like another tech rabbit hole to me."

"I hear that," Ramon says. "That's why I'm seeing Jade. She'll know if this is something to pursue."

I nod. "Good. If we're going into something like this, I need to know it's—"

"—a sure thing?" Ramon says, grinning at his own callback to the kid's pitch. I laugh.

"Exactly," I say.

"You know," Ramon says, "Jade's a friend of my wife. If you wanted to join me on the drinks…"

I roll my eyes at his lack of subtlety. "Are you trying to set me up, Ramon?"

He holds up his hands. "Guilty. But only if you want me to, boss."

"I'm still technically married," I remind him.

"We both know that's not what's stopping you," he says. "But if you say you're not into it, I respect that."

What I want to tell him is that the last thing I need is to be set up with his wife's friend who, I can guarantee, is looking for a relationship—something I've effectively sworn off. Sex without strings is the only way I want to operate.

"I appreciate it," I say, thanking God that our elevator's finally opening up on the floor. And I do. Ramon's a good guy, even if he's pushing for something that'll never happen.

"Good morning, Mr. Duke," Sandy says with a smile, handing me a cup of coffee. "Ready for a busy day of taking over the world?"

I chuckle. "You make me sound so nefarious."

"I meant it in a good way," she says with a wink. "The *good* kind of taking over the world. Now, are you ready for me to brief you on your schedule for the day?"

She gives me the rundown of the day, the meetings I'm expected in and the calls I'll need to make. I nod, letting business cover my mind, erasing all thoughts of Emery.

That is, until I see her. She's in the conference room, sitting in a chair with a notebook in her lap. She's being diligent, the pen moving across the page as she looks from speaker to speaker.

"Sandy, who's meeting in the conference room right now?"

Sandy glances past me to the room.

"Hm, looks like marketing," Sandy says. "I didn't book you. Should I have?"

Normally, I don't go to the marketing meetings. It's a well-oiled part of the machine, one I spent a lot of time to make sure it could run smoothly without me. I get emails with meeting notes after, and it's just not something I normally have a lot of thoughts on. I've hired the best, and they don't need me.

"No, Sandy, it's fine," I say. "But I might pop in and see how it's going."

I tell myself that I'm not thinking with my dick. It wouldn't hurt to pay more attention to marketing. I live and breathe for this company, after all. I'm going to just check out the meeting and remind myself that Emery is not what I need. A closer look will remind me that she's an intern, nothing more than another girl trying to make it in the big city, and not worth another thought.

I stride across the office until I reach the conference room and push my way inside. A few of the executives cast me wide-eyed glances, including Katiyah, my head of marketing.

"Mr. Duke," Katiyah says. "To what do we owe this lovely surprise?"

"Nothing to worry about, Katiyah," I say, offering her a smile. "I just thought I'd drop in. Carry on."

I wave off a chair when it's offered. I prefer to stand near the door, leaning against the wall as I cross my arms. I sweep the room with my gaze. Katiyah jumps right back into her presentation, lowering the lights so she can project her PowerPoint for the group. It's something about the latest app we're launching, but I'm only pretending to listen.

Instead, I'm watching her. Emery. She's still taking notes and hasn't glanced in my direction, but I can feel that it's an effort. She brings the pen to her mouth, tracing her bottom lip. The image of her doing that same motion with my dick makes me harden. I can envision her bent over my bed with her hands tied above her head, blindfolded, as I made her moan my name. She'd beg to reciprocate until I let her take my cock in her mouth. She'd need to be taught, and I'd relish the teaching, showing her exactly what I like. How to tease me with her tongue before taking me in her mouth. How hard to suck while pumping me with her hand and swirling her tongue. I'd take that squeaky-clean image of hers and dirty it up so thoroughly she'd never come again without thinking of me.

This little fantasy is so filthy that I have to look away lest I get a full erection right here in the middle of the meeting, dimmed lights or not.

Still, I can't keep my eyes off of her for long. I'm like an addict, needing another hit, another glance. I want her to notice me too. I want her to look at me.

After a minute, she does look. Her eyes slide to me, not their usual wide-eyed bunny look, but half-lidded, like she can see right into my naughty thoughts. And even if she does see through me, she doesn't look away. Instead, she holds my eye contact for several seconds, biting her lip a bit before she smiles.

What the hell? This isn't the doe-eyed girl from lunch yesterday. I know what that smile means. Did she read some kind of self-help seduction book last night or a fucking *Seventeen* magazine?

I leave the meeting. I don't need this kind of confusion. I was ready to let her go, but now, she's burned into my brain, even when I'm back in my office. All I can think about is if she could keep that smile on her lips with my face between her legs. Somehow, I doubt she could.

CHAPTER EIGHT

FOR THE REST of the morning, I seriously consider jacking off in my office. I can't get the picture of Emery's lips out of my mind. But unfortunately—or fortunately, depending on how I decide to look at it—I've got a full morning booked, and business thankfully manages to push some of my filthy thoughts to the side. But by the time the afternoon rolls around, I'm itching with excess energy that I need to blow off.

I decide to take a closer look at some of the materials that Monica sent over about Pink. Samples and descriptions of porn that, as she said, cater to a woman's sexual desire. I decide to pull up a clip from one, and even though it feels insanely inappropriate, the reality is that I'm actually doing my job.

It's the description that makes me want to click. A story about a girl from a quiet midwestern town, lost and looking for love. It feels too familiar and, fuck it, let's be honest—like Emery. I want to see what Monica's people think a girl like Emery wants.

It's just a clip, and it starts in a kitchen. A girl's at her table when a man walks in who's there to fix her washer. It feels exactly like every other cliché porn I've ever watched, and I'm actually disappointed in Monica.

Except, then, instead of bending her over and fucking the girl senseless, the man drops to his knees and lets her wrap her legs around his head. He licks her until she's screaming, the chair actually falling over as she shakes with pleasure. Then, and only then, does he move to enter her.

Of course, that's where the clip cuts off. It is just a sample. But I see what Monica meant. If this were a man's porn, the foreplay would've been the first to go, and a woman's oral pleasure certainly wouldn't take up such prime real estate. There's also the way it was shot, with focus on the man's body rather than just on the woman's.

It's interesting, but unfortunately, it's not the kind of business that takes my mind off a certain Kansan. Instead, it makes me wonder, is this the sort of fantasy she was talking about? Because I'd be up for the task.

It's exactly the wrong thing to be thinking about. I get up to take a walk in order to shake off my blue balls and get my mind reoriented. Not outside, just around the office. One thing about the marketing meeting is that it did remind me that I've gotten into a routine the past few months, especially after my marriage fell apart. I haven't been as involved as I like to be.

And, fuck it, I'm not delusional. I know I'm looking for an excuse to run into *her*. I know that's not likely to happen if I never leave my own office.

I weave my way through the main office, past the conference room and the executive offices. It's fairly quiet and I realize it's already midday and most likely everyone is out taking in the nice New York weather, out for lunch. I don't mind. Business often happens outside these walls, and all I care about is that the money ends up back here.

I'm about to head back to my own office when I hear voices. A high, tinkly laugh.

Her.

I'm pretty sure it's coming from a janitor's closet. I wonder who she's in there with and feel a flash of unjustified and unwarranted jealousy. I should walk away. How many times do I have to tell myself to walk away? Fucking ridiculous.

Instead, I push open the door. Turns out, it's not a janitor's closet. It's a kitchenette where, apparently, coffee comes from. There's a row of mugs, a microwave, a few coffeepots, a fridge. Emery's holding a mug in one hand as she chats with Sandy. Both of them look a little wide-eyed at the sight of me, but I have to imagine for very different reasons.

I exhale, pretty sure my shoulders visibly drop with the breath leaving my body. God, I'm an idiot. Emery's in here laughing with my assistant, not some twenty-something from accounting. Or say, my best friend.

"Oh, Mr. Duke, I'm sorry," Sandy says. "I didn't realize you needed something. I could've brought it for you if you'd buzzed."

Of course she would have. I didn't even know this kitchenette existed. It really wouldn't hurt me to get out of my own office more, apparently.

"No need, Sandy." I smile, like finding my own coffee is normal. "I thought I'd stretch my legs. That last meeting has me a bit wound up."

I don't mention that I was watching work-related porn in my office.

Sandy smiles. "You work too hard, sir."

I shrug. "The only way to get anything done."

Sandy laughs, exchanging a look with Emery. "I better get back to my desk. It was nice chatting with you, Emery. You let me know if you have any more questions."

She leaves us in the kitchenette where we are dangerously alone. The door slowly shuts, on one of those hydraulic hinges that ensures the door will close without slamming.

When it finally clicks into place, firmly shut, it feels like an hour has passed but logically I think it's been about thirty seconds. Maybe forty-five.

I've used all of them to examine Emery. Her lips look bee-stung and supple, practically begging to be kissed. She'd pulled her hair into another high pony, exposing her neck, a silver necklace disappearing into her cleavage. I force myself to meet her eyes with difficulty.

"So, interviewing my assistant now, are you?" I ask.

"I was just talking to her," Emery says with a defensive shrug and a surprised blink. "Is that a problem?"

"I wasn't implying anything," I say. "Though, if you wanted to know about me, you could've just asked."

She laughs. "Oh, you assume I was asking about you?"

I step closer to her. "Weren't you?"

The blush on her face is answer enough. She was asking about me. And now, I'm making her cheeks darken. Her chest rises as her breathing increases just a fraction. I wonder what other effect I'm having on her. I wonder if she's wet and achy.

Heat spikes down my spine, thick and molten. It's one thing to imagine her and a completely different thing to be here in her presence. One step and I could have her in my arms.

I can't think about that. I'll just get a mug. Exactly. I'll just grab a coffee and then I'll be on my way. Nothing inappropriate about that. Just. A fucking. Coffee. I lean past her to grab a mug. My hand brushes the bare skin of her arm, sending an electric shot up and down my body.

I pause, hand on the shelf and evaluate.

It's nothing. I can still leave. Except, just as I'm about to pull my arm back, she stops me. She stops me by...kissing me. She has to fist my shirt to tug me a bit closer and press up on her toes in order to reach. Her lips find mine in a kitten-sweet kiss. Her lips are sinfully soft, twin pillows that press against mine.

And then it's over. So fast I wonder if I'm hallucinating. I do work too much. My stress level is far too high.

I straighten and look at her, harder than likely necessary. "What the hell was that?"

She falters, confidence dropping. Then produces a tiny defiant glare. "A kiss, obviously. Unless I was too forward?"

"That wasn't a kiss," I growl.

"Yes it—"

I cut her off, moving in one swift motion so that she's pinned against the counter. She lets out a delicious gasp as I do, immediately pressing forward so that her breasts are pressed flush against my chest. My cock swells in response and there's no way she's missing the effect she has on me.

"I think this is what you meant to do," I tell her, crushing my mouth to hers. I hear the shatter of the coffee mug that she was holding as she slides her arms around my neck, pulling me impossibly closer. A whimper is caught in her throat as she digs one hand into my hair. The thought that someone might hear the mug breaking flickers across my mind, but fuck it.

Fuck it. I own the company. Plus, her lips. There's no logical thought to be had in this room, in this universe beyond her lips. Her tongue gingerly probes, sweet and insistent. I groan against her as she winds her fingers into my hair and tugs.

"If you weren't my intern..." I say, grabbing her throat.

She pulls back from the kiss, red-faced with her pink lipstick smeared. One kiss, and already, she looks undone. Her breathing heavy, full of lust. Yes, I bet that pussy's wet for me. I could have her right here if I wanted.

"What would you do?" she asks, the question an eager combination of seductive and curious that is quintessentially Emery.

I kiss her again, harder, biting her lower lip. I trace another kiss down her jaw, enjoying the way she shivers against me.

"We could really have some fun," I say, nipping at her throat as she moans.

"What…kind of fun?" she asks, need heavy in her voice.

"The kinky-as-hell kind," I promise, kissing her hard again, my hand coming up to cup her breast, my thumb brushing across her nipple. She's perfect. The weight of her in my hand, her nipple rock hard under my thumb. Perfectly malleable through her thin blouse, and she shudders again as she grinds forward against me.

"Tell me," she begs. "Tell me what we'd do."

I plan to tell her, but first, I'll give her a taste. I kiss her harder before taking full advantage of her low-cut blouse, sliding my fingers into her bra, working her nipple between my fingers. I trail my lips across her jaw before twisting her nipple, lightly, but enough. Enough to make her gasp. Enough that I can feel the heat of her pussy as I grip her ass and pull her tighter against me.

I'm about to elaborate on exactly what kind of fun we could have, every filthy detail, when suddenly, I hear voices. They're just outside, plus the click of heels. Fuck. Of course. In the moment, I forgot that the office might be relatively quiet, but not for long.

I push back from her and away from the door as she straightens her blouse, just in time as Ramon and one of Blythe's executives walk in. They look confused when they see me, though Ramon's wide eyes tells me he knows exactly what was just happening.

"Oh, I'll get this, uh, cleaned up," Emery says, her face a bright red as she bends over to search for a dust pan in the cabinets. As she starts to sweep the ceramic shards, my eyes immediately trace the outline of her firm ass, and it takes Ramon clearing his throat for me to remember where I am.

Fuck. I'm thinking with my dick, and this absolutely will not stand.

"Call maintenance," I say, and then I turn, leaving both the girl and the mess behind me.

CHAPTER NINE

IT CAN'T HAPPEN AGAIN. That, I know. Ever since the incident in the kitchenette the other day, Ramon's been smirking at me nonstop, saying bullshit like, "So, that's why you weren't interested in Jade." Thankfully, he's out today with a client, not waiting around to press me for details. Still, even without him, no amount of work gets the girl out of my mind, and no amount of jacking off, either. If anything, my fantasies about her are getting more desperate.

If HR knew, they'd be up my ass in a second. The power dynamic's all wrong. I'm her boss. She's an intern. She takes notes. I own the place. I need to move on and get her out of my head.

She's not made it easy, either. She's started walking by me whenever she can in clothes that seem to get tighter and skirts that get shorter, batting her eyelashes at me. Then, there are the moments I catch her unaware, like yesterday when we were walking to the same elevator. She looked up, and there it was, the innocent Kansas girl with the doe eyes. Pure. Sweet. But quickly replaced by those half-lidded eyes and a step toward me. I had to pretend that I'd forgotten something in my office to extricate myself from the moment.

Who is she? A minx one moment, an innocent kitten the next.

Who am I? The CEO one moment, taking inane detours to avoid her the next.

There has been one highlight to the week. Blythe has been surprisingly silent for a few days. Maybe she finally got it through her head that I won't be caving to her manipulation this time.

"Mr. Duke? I've got some bad news."

I look up and see Sandy's popped her head into my office. I must have been so wrapped up in my thoughts that I didn't hear her come in.

"Bad news?" I ask. "Don't tell me those contracts to Tokyo didn't make it out."

Sandy laughs. "Oh, no, not that. In fact, it's not really bad news to anyone except you."

I cock my eyebrow at her. Sandy knows I don't like to be teased about business.

Her face falls a little. "You really did forget, didn't you? The charity auction tomorrow?"

Oh, fuck. Of course I forgot. Anything to do with the charity is tied to Blythe, meaning I prefer not to touch it with a ten-foot pole.

"You can't back out," Sandy says, cutting me off before I can say anything. "All your major clients will be there. They'll expect to see you. In fact, they'll want to see you. You're probably the only reason they paid such exorbitant table fees to attend."

She's stroking my ego. It shouldn't be that easy, but it is. Plus, Sandy's basically been keeping my life afloat these past few months. Okay, years. I won't fight her on it.

"Right," I say with a resigned sigh. "Fine. As long as you'll be there to remind me who I need to thank and for what. And politely interrupt anyone taking up too much of my time. You know I can't be trusted at these things on my own."

"Ah," Sandy says. "So you forgot that part, too. The part that makes it *really* bad news."

"Sandy…" I warn.

"I told you weeks ago that I can't be there," she says. "I'm flying home for a family wedding."

"But I can't do it by myself," I remind her. "I never remember who donated what and I have no patience for small talk."

Truthfully, this was one of Blythe's strengths. At any event we went to, she was able to remember not just who we were talking to, but their kids, their likes, their dislikes, the way they liked their meat prepared—everything. I was able to coast along as she whispered important snippets in my ears, taking each one and spinning it back with my charm. But without Blythe, Sandy had to step in. Thankfully, it worked out. She was good, thorough. Without her, I'll be completely adrift.

"I've arranged a substitute," Sandy says. "The new intern, Emery. She's an excellent note taker and has a terrific memory. I've been quizzing her all week on the details, and I'm sure she'll be just perfect."

It takes a lot of effort to keep my mouth from falling open.

"There must be other options," I say. "Anyone."

"You don't like Emery?" Sandy says, frowning. "Everyone else thinks she's sweet as pie. Charming. And besides excellent at schmoozing."

"No, it's not that," I say, searching for a lie. "It's just—"

"I know she had that issue with the coffee," Sandy says, "but we all have clumsy moments, and I promise, she'll do a great job. And if not, we can fire her."

Damn. Sandy's got a cold streak behind that winning smile.

"That won't be necessary," I say. "I was just caught off guard."

"I understand, Mr. Duke," Sandy says. "I already gave Leo her address and told her what time to be ready. And remember, smile! You own the world."

"I thought I was taking it over," I say, remembering our earlier conversation.

"Same thing," she says with a wink. "I'm headed out now. Think you can handle the office on your own for the rest of the day?"

I shrug. "Don't really have a choice, do I?"

She smiles. "You're a good boss, Mr. Duke. I'll see you Monday."

I let out a frustrated sigh as soon as the door closes behind Sandy. It's not her fault that she's orchestrated the most frustrating complication of my life for tomorrow. She has no idea I'm having trouble sleeping without dreams of Emery Mills invading my thoughts. She doesn't know a thing about the kitchenette incident.

Not that any of it matters. In this situation, I just have to be professional, which is certainly something I can manage.

And, in the meantime, there are still a few hours left in the day to be productive.

I need to make a copy of a contract I want Ramon to review and rather than wait for Sandy, I decide to do it myself. Sure, it's been a while since I made a copy, but I'm not an idiot. I'll figure it out.

I head to the copy room, finding it empty. Good. I put some of the papers in and then hover over the buttons, trying to decide what to push. Fucking complicated machines.

"I could help you with that, you know," someone purrs behind me.

Fuck. Even before I turn around, I know it's Emery because I cannot catch a break. Her perfume's heavy today, not her usual rose scent. It's something sweet and almost citrusy. I turn around, and find her watching me, a hand on her hip and God help me, from where I'm standing I can see the hint of a black lacy bra peeking out, cradling her perfect tits. Jesus Christ.

"Thanks," I manage, my tone dismissive. "But I think I'm capable of doing this myself."

"Oh," she says, dragging out the word, "I wasn't talking about the copies."

Fucking hell.

I can feel her step closer. Much closer. I know she's moved directly behind me. She lays a tentative hand on my back.

I fight every urge I have not to take advantage of what she's clearly trying to offer. My dick does not appreciate my sudden onset of morals.

"That won't be necessary," I say, stepping away from her. Which might have been enough to end it if I wasn't stupid enough to look at her.

She's blushing, and confused. Which I suppose is fair since I had my hand in her blouse only a few days ago.

"Have I upset you?" Emery asks, stepping again towards me. "If I have," she pauses, biting into her bottom lip while she seems to contemplate her next words or gather her courage. Her eyes flicker to mine and away and back again. "You could always…spank me."

She says the final two words so softly I wonder if I even heard her correctly or if I'm hallucinating. I shake off a laugh of surprise as it hits me that I've read her completely wrong. This is no innocent farm girl from Kansas, though she played one very, very well. This is a girl who's interested in playing. And if that's the case, well, who am I to stand in her way?

In a few steps, I've backed her into a tall filing cabinet next to the copier. She lets out a delighted squeak as I pin her wrists above her head with one of my hands.

"You're playing with fire," I warn, letting my other hand glide over her hip to that firm and supple ass. I give it a tight squeeze. In response, she leans forward and presses her lips close to my ear.

"Am I?" Emery whispers, her lips brushing against my cheek. I can feel her heart racing, her chest pressed against mine. "Maybe I like fire?" she adds, but it comes out like a question not a statement and her breath catches.

I smile, impressed with her moxie as I keep my hand moving, stroking the curve of her ass, slowly into the curve of her thigh. She's in a skirt. It wouldn't take much to slide a finger inside of her. Into the wetness that I know waits for me. The wetness for me. I could tease the nerves there, could have her moaning and tightening around my fingers with both of us still fully dressed. Or I could bend her over that blasted copier and give her the spanking she requested. Slap her tight ass straight into orgasm.

As if reading my mind, she wraps one leg around me and pulls me closer, grinding against me. She wants me, right here, right now.

"You don't know what you're asking for," I say.

"Probably not," she laughs a little when she says it, the curve of her lips pressing against my neck. "Which is exactly why you need to give it to me, please."

Oh, fuck. I'm so damn hard against her, and it wouldn't take much to hike that skirt around her hips. I'm dying to slide inside her, to be skin to skin. I could do it. I know she's wet for me. Know she wants it as badly as I do.

Except, what the hell am I doing? There's not even a door here. I'm practically asking for an HR nightmare. I step back and drop my hands to the side.

This is insanity.

The only way I might even consider it—and *might* is a strong word—is if she pursues me. If she keeps begging for it, then I'll drag her off to my office and fuck her until she screams. But I won't play this game. I won't beg her. She'll ask, or that'll be the end of it.

I watch her catch her breath against the filing cabinet. She's staring me down, those eyes wide again, like she's trying to figure me out.

Finally, after a moment, she straightens her skirt and re-buttons her top.

"I wouldn't have minded more," she says at last, clicking her heels away from me and down the hall.

Minded? I'm stuck with blue balls and she says she wouldn't have "minded"? There's something about this girl, but I don't know what it is. She makes no sense and is a walking contradiction. A scalding hot contradiction, but still.

Fuck the copies. They can wait until Sandy's back. And my dick can wait for, I don't know for what. But it can wait. I'm not a goddamn teenager with a hard-on. Still, I'm locking myself in my office, and I won't leave until I know that girl's gone home for the day. Which, of course, doesn't solve tomorrow's problem.

But that's an issue that's just going to have to wait.

CHAPTER TEN

"LEO, where the hell are we going?"

"To pick up Ms. Mills, sir."

Right. Right, Ms. Mills. "This is one hell of a neighborhood," I mutter from the back seat, like the out-of-touch asshole that I am.

"She's an intern, sir." Leo returns without a hint of the sarcasm I deserve for expecting interns to have a better address.

"It's not a date," I add, not that he's asked.

"Yes, sir," Leo says, nodding with understanding.

Even though it doesn't matter—Leo is discreet as they come—I feel the need to explain.

"Sandy was supposed to join me, but she couldn't, so this girl's filling in," I say. "The one I took to lunch the other day. She's just a colleague."

Leo smiles. "Of course, sir."

I can tell he doesn't believe me, even though he should. It's not like I'm picking up interns left and right. All of my dates since Blythe have been age appropriate. Not that there have been many dates. More like one-night stands. Still, the point is, it's not like picking up interns is a habit of mine.

Then again, maybe I'm misinterpreting the twinkle in the old man's eye. Or maybe I'm imagining it entirely.

I'm too in my head. That's the problem. What happened between me and Emery at the copy machine has me rattled, and I need to put it aside. Sandy's right about tonight, after all. I'll be at my highest level of visibility with our most high-profile clients. Not to mention that Blythe will definitely be there, and it's important that I look like I'm on top of the world. Not worried. Not bothered. In control, always.

Emery's place is only about fifteen blocks from mine, but it might as well be in another state. Another world. Yet, I can't help thinking that Emery must love it. How each neighborhood in New York is a world unto its own. She can walk in her little kitten heels a few blocks and find something different every day. A different universe compared to Kansas, which must surely be acres upon acres of barns.

God, I'm a dick.

There's likely a few strip malls and Walmarts there too.

Emery's building is beige-colored with rickety, rusted fire escapes running down the front. There's a Dollar Discount store one building over. The formerly gold letters announcing the building numbers are faded, one of them missing completely.

"Will you be going up to get the lady?" Leo asks, glancing at me in the mirror.

I had planned on texting her to come down, but something about Leo's tone tells me that he expects me to be a gentleman and go into this fire hazard of a building to fetch Emery. I sigh, knowing he's right. Manners matter, even when it's not a date. And Emery deserves to be picked up at her door, even if this is strictly professional. Something I need to keep reminding myself.

"Of course," I say, stepping out of the car.

I press unit 3 from the options on the door outside while a

passing dog walker gives me and my suit a curious look. If anyone's ever been out of place on this street, it's me. I'd hazard a guess that my suit probably cost at least a month's worth of rent in this place, maybe two. The thought makes me uneasy.

The door buzzes, letting me into a lobby that smells like old carpet and dust. There're mailboxes on one side with names pasted above each number. Names jotted down in sharpie and slapped to the wall with packing tape, or in one case, a staple gun. There's obviously no greeter waiting to guide me to the elevators. In fact, there's one elevator, period, and it's broken, which is just as well. An elevator in a building like this is likely to break down, stuck between floors. Stairs, it is.

It's fine. I'm a fit man. I can handle a few stairs. I head up to her unit and find that the paint on the door is chipped. I knock. Within seconds, the door's flung open, and there she is.

Fuck. All of today, I told myself that she's nothing, just the shiny new plaything at the office, someone fun to flirt with to take the edge off of business. I reasoned that this must be some deep fantasy of mine surfacing about innocent farm girls, probably some porn I watched as a teen that buried itself deep in my brain and has now been reactivated by the arrival of Emery and her clumsy, coffee-spilling, dainty hands. The desire to push her back against the wall of my office and drive my cock inside her until she sees stars is purely primal lust that'll fade away once something else captures my attention. I'm a grown man, a business man, fuck, a billionaire of my own making. I am capable of forget-ting this girl.

I'm also deluded. Clearly fucking deluded. I know that the moment she opens the door.

She is a star, blinking in the sky, beckoning me forward. When I see her, everything else falls away, and there's nothing but her, dragging me into her orbit, urging me to fall deeper and deeper into her abyss.

It doesn't help that she's dressed up for the occasion in a form-fitting navy dress that dips low to reveal her chest and swishes above her knees. She's wearing strappy, gold heels that show off her legs, but the worst part by far is that she's pulled her hair back. This way, I can see her slender neck, her pink cheeks, and her bright brown eyes. They're settling on me now, working their way down until she's looked at every part of me. She lingers below my abdomen, and I wonder if she's imagining unbuttoning my belt. She bites her lip, and now I don't have to wonder. She *is* thinking about me. Does she want me to throw her up against a wall right here in her apartment? I wonder what she has on—or not—underneath that little dress.

"Mr. Duke," she says in a breathy voice that makes my cock jump against the fabric of my pants. "I didn't expect you to come to the door."

"I have manners," I say, even though my gruff voice probably reveals all of the decidedly not-mannerly things that I want to do to her.

"Of course," she says with a little laugh, batting her long eyelashes at me. "Do you want the tour?"

No. I don't want to take another step inside this apartment. Closer quarters will not serve me or this situation well.

"Come on," she insists. "I feel like I need to prove to you that it isn't…what did you call it? A shithole?"

I grimace, but she opens the door wider and waves me inside. Immediately, I'm certain that I have closets in my apartment that are bigger than this place. The kitchen and the living room spill over into one another, and both are loaded with hand-me-down, bohemian-style furniture. There's a framed poster of Paris that I'd bet was bought on a street corner in New York, and the blanket thrown over the sofa looks like it was handmade, and not by someone who knew what they were doing.

"I live with two roommates," she says. "So it's really a steal. And see, out that window? You can see the park."

"Which park?" I ask, squinting to try to make out what she's talking about.

"Carl Schurz," she tells me, as if that means anything. From the window, all I can see is a few trees and maybe a bench. "I like to go running there."

I immediately attempt to blot out the image of Emery in spandex, jogging. But my brain has already told me to fuck off and my eyes are taking another perusal of her tits in that dress.

Not Appropriate.

Besides, this tiny apartment is a glaring reminder of something else. Emery is not of my world. She's an intern, freshly graduated from college. She barely owns real furniture. She can barely even afford to be in New York, even with roommates. Anything beyond a professional work relationship with this girl would be beyond inappropriate and a one-way ticket to a lecture from my own HR department, or worse, a lawsuit. Plus, she deserves to date a guy with his own run-down apartment, someone who she can bond with over free concerts in the park or whatever the fuck normal people bond over. *Remember,* I tell myself, *this is a girl who's surely dreaming about the perfect guy to carry her away into the sunset, not a quick fuck with her boss.*

So why do I keep forgetting all of those things?

"We should really get going," I insist, checking my watch to drive the point home. "We don't want to be late."

"Oh," she says, looking vaguely put out. "Are you sure you don't want to see the rest?"

She blushes and avoids looking at me. Dear God, what is going on with this girl? One minute, she's propositioning me in the copier room, the next she's fidgeting like I'm her prom date and her parents are out of town.

My phone buzzes, and I look down. It's Leo asking if he should do some laps or wait for me. I text him back that we're heading down now.

"I'm sure," I say, and I am. The last thing I need is a visual memory of her bedroom which I'd only use to jack off to. I turn and head out of her apartment before she can argue. "I bet it's lovely though."

She hesitates, looking back towards her bedroom before shrugging and following me and now I'm questioning if she was hoping for a quickie before the event.

I'm also questioning why the fuck I wouldn't take her up on it.

"Fine," she says. "You win. Let's go."

She locks up—with me keeping a healthy distance down the hall—and then we head down to the car. I slide in after her, and thankfully, she stays safely on her side of the back seat. She's pinned to the window for the drive, staring out at the lights that blink and shine across town.

"It's such a beautiful city," she says. "Don't you think?"

I don't indulge her this time. If I'm going to keep my distance, I'm going to really need to keep my distance. She needs to understand that this is professional and that I have things at stake.

"Did you bring something to take notes with?" I ask, since it's the only thing I can think of.

She laughs. "Uh, my phone?"

"Right," I say. "I guess your little notebook would be out of place. But it's important that you pay attention tonight. Clients drop hints about what they want, how they're feeling. It's important that we—you—stay on top of these things."

She smiles. "Don't worry. I can be...on top of things."

A poor choice of words, and she knows it. It immediately stirs up the image in my mind of her on top of me, straddling me with those beautiful thighs. I could suck on her nipples as she rode me, all the way straight through to orgasm.

"What's the event for, anyway?" Emery asks, breaking the image. "Sandy didn't say."

It's a boner killer of a question, and I'm grateful. Because this is a charity event, and as it's a charity event, that means Blythe is in charge. Which means I stay the hell away from it.

"Charity auction," I say. "Blythe's running it."

"Your wife," Emery murmurs.

"Nearly ex," I snap before the word *wife* is completely out of her mouth, then shake my head in irritation with myself. Blythe's status in my life is as irrelevant as Emery's. What Emery thinks of Blythe's existence is unimportant. If anything I should be playing up the wife angle to keep Emery at arm's length. *Wife, wife, wife.*

Yet. My mouth remains closed.

"Which charity?" Emery finally asks after a bit of a pause in which she stares at my profile while I stare at my conscience.

I shrug. "I don't know."

"Oh," she says. She looks like there's more she wants to say, but she doesn't. Instead, she returns to looking out of her window.

I'm glad she doesn't force more conversation, particularly since I'm not eager to talk about Blythe. My skin's already crawling with the thought that I'll have to see her tonight.

"We're here," Leo calls from the driver's seat. I slide out and hold the door, holding my hand out for Emery. She takes it gingerly, shivering at my touch. I let go as soon as she's got both feet on the ground.

Her eyes are wider than usual as she looks at the Hilton before us. Wide columns reach high up into New York's night sky, and the walkway is flooded with people in their finest suits and dresses. Cameras flash nearby, and there's a bustle of excitement as people walk inside.

This is business, I remind myself for the thousandth time. *Not pleasure.*

Thus, no need to enjoy her excitement. No need to catalog the blush on her cheeks or the way she smooths her fingers over the shell of her ear to check for loose tendrils of hair.

Absolutely zero point in noticing any of it.

Once we're inside the lavishly decorated event hall, we take laps around the room to check out all of the various items and experiences that are being auctioned off. Each of our clients has offered something valuable up, from signed hockey sticks to rare Hollywood memorabilia. Lunch with a celebrity or a trip to Tahiti. Emery takes to bouncing from item to item and staring, openmouthed, back at me when she sees the price tag on the item.

"Ten thousand dollars," she says, pointing at a silvery dress. "All because some starlet wore it to the Oscars."

"It'll go for much more than that," I tell her. "And remember, this is for charity."

Emery raises an eyebrow. "A charity you don't even know."

"I do now," I say, pointing to the banner hanging above the auction items. "New York Children's Welfare."

Emery scrunches up her nose. "And what sort of welfare do they provide?"

"I don't know," I say honestly. "As I said, this is—"

"Your ex-wife's project," Emery fills in. "I just thought..."

Her voice trails off, and her doe eyes find the floor before looking back at me. There's something she wants to say, but the tightrope of our relationship is stopping her. I don't know whether to be annoyed or relieved. She certainly didn't have any problem voicing her opinions before.

Yet.

"You thought what?" I prod.

"Never mind," she says. "Shouldn't we be chatting with some clients?"

She's right, of course. That's why I'm here. I can't be wasting time talking about the charity itself. After all, it makes no difference to me what charity Blythe's picked out, especially since I know that lately Blythe's turned it into a funnel for her and my asshole of an ex-best friend. The less I know, the better.

We make our way around the room, chatting with clients, finding out how they're doing. Emery's an excellent swap in for Sandy, and honestly, she handles the conversations with the same sort of easy charm that Blythe used to. Plus, where Blythe's charm was all manipulation and false interest, Emery actually seems to give a damn about what each person's saying. She's talking to one old guy about his grandchildren for so long that I practically have to yank her away.

"We'll follow up later," she tells the older gentleman. "And I'll be in touch about your idea for the new product marketing."

"Oh, you will?" I ask when we're far enough away. "I didn't realize that was your job."

She laughs, shrugging as she jots another note to herself on her phone before looking up at me. "Honestly, it just felt like the right thing to say. And I'll make sure someone does follow up with him. It was a good idea."

Maybe it was. For once in my life, I wasn't focused on business. While she was talking to him, all I could focus on was her, the way her laugh lights up her entire face and how she kept tucking a loose hair behind her ear.

An announcement fills the room, telling us all it's time to place our final bids and get to our seats for the dinner. We're moved along by the crowd, everyone heading off to their table.

We head in, a chill zipping up and down my spine when we reach our table.

Of course she would do this. How could I have expected anything less?

There, at the table near the front, is Blythe, wearing a slinky black dress with little jewels at the neckline, holding her glass of champagne as if she owns the damn room. For anyone looking on, nothing's wrong. She's certainly not a woman in the middle of a contentious divorce. She isn't a life ruiner or a friend fucker. She's Blythe Lawrence-Duke, belle of the fucking ball.

And at her side? Her newest partner, gazing up at her with his trademark smirk. Her partner in crime, literally. And my ex-best friend.

Next to me, I feel Emery's presence as she steps forward. She's clearly seeing the same thing I am, and she bites her lip at the sight. I watch as Blythe's eyes slide over to us, catching us in her cold smile even as she carries on conversation with the others at the table.

She's set a trap, and she knows it. I can't exactly tell her to fuck off in front of our clients and business associates. I'll have to play nice, and playing nice with her will no doubt end with a heaping helping of her signature manipulation.

"So, I could be wrong," Emery says next to me, drawing me back to her. "But does the CEO actually have to eat at this thing?"

I raise my eyebrow at her.

"I'm just wondering," she says. "I mean, we did what you came here to do, right? We cozied up with the clients, and I've got lots of great information for Monday. Is the dinner part… totally necessary?"

She says it so innocently, her mouth turned up in the smallest pout as she shrugs. I stare at her, almost laughing at the ludicrous suggestion.

"Leave the event now?" I ask, just to make sure I'm understanding her.

"Well, yeah. Besides," she says, moving so close to whisper in my ear that I can feel the heat of her skin radiating through the fabric of our clothes, "don't you own everything? If you wanted to leave, who would be able to tell you no?"

A different kind of trap. The delicious kind. The words are thick with insinuation, reminding me of just how easy it would be to check into a room upstairs for a few hours and have my way with her. To burn away the sight of Blythe and that asshole with a good fuck.

But I can't do that. I have to maintain this boundary. No matter how tempted I might be.

Still, as I glance back at Blythe, an alternative venue might not be such a bad idea. Emery's right that I've done the necessary mingling. Dinner somewhere else might be the perfect compromise to the shitty situation that Blythe's forced me into.

"I wouldn't mind finding somewhere else to eat," I tell Emery, turning my back on Blythe.

"Great," Emery says, her lips curving into a smile. "Because I'm starving, and I know just the right place."

CHAPTER ELEVEN

IT TURNS out that Emery's idea for dinner is far closer than I could have imagined. As soon as we're outside in the cool night air, she waves away my offer to call Leo, insisting we can walk with a little grin.

"It's the best," she says. "I swear. I've never had anything like it before."

I'd bet that there are a lot of things the girl's never had anything like before, but I don't say it. Instead, I watch as she waits patiently like a tourist for the light to change, vibrating with energy and enthusiasm about this dinner. And when I follow her across the street I have to admit that walking has its merits. Mainly the view of Emery's ass.

"Ta-da!" she squeals. "Dinner."

"Where?" I ask, because all we've done is cross the street. We're damn near still in the intersection of 53rd and 6th and there aren't any restaurants on this corner. There's a Starbucks, thankfully closed because I'm not eating dinner there —and not much else.

But she doesn't answer me. She hurries forward, her heels clicking on the pavement and her grin infectious as she flashes it at me over her shoulder.

"They have the best falafel," she says. "I'd never even had falafel before I moved here, but now I love it, and this place is by far the best."

Falafel? I scan the street again, and finally, I see what she's talking about. A tiny food cart and two lone guys manning it, the words "The Halal Guys" printed on the side of the cart.

"You've got to be kidding me," I say, but she's still grinning as she hooks her arm in mine and drags me to the end of the line. "You want to eat dinner on the street? From a food cart?" It's quite an operation, I'll admit. If one enjoys eating dinner served out of a cart while leaning against a building or perched on a cement planter.

Which I do not. Or at least I don't think I do, because it's not something I'd normally do.

"Now, I'm just going to suggest that you at least get a side of falafel," she says. "It's that good. But get whatever you want. The bowls are awesome, and so are the gyros... honestly, it's all good. You can't go wrong. I promise you."

I stare at her. I've never seen someone this excited about a fucking food cart in my life. She waved her hands when pledging that promise that I'll love it and honesty—I'm also sure no one has made such an earnest promise to me in my entire life.

So here I am—standing in line to buy street food while my five-hundred-dollar-a-plate charity dinner goes untouched just a few New York feet away.

And yet. Nothing on Earth could compel me to abandon this spontaneous dinner and head back inside.

I order the chicken platter for myself while Emery selects a gyro sandwich, with a four piece side of falafel, and an order of fries, telling me we'll share. Then she pauses, her tongue darting out to wet her bottom lip, to clarify. We'll share the falafel, she tells me. If I want fries I should order my own. The food is ready at the exact speed you'd expect from a food truck. Wrapped and ready nearly as fast as I can pass a couple of twenties to pay for it. As I'm pocketing the change, preparing to fire off a text to Leo to have him come pick us up, she steps past me and lowers her ass— fancy dress and all—onto a cement planter, unwraps the sandwich, and takes the largest bite I've ever seen a woman take.

She glances at me mid-bite and swallows. "What? You think I'm going to wait to eat this? You have to eat it while it's still hot."

I look around at the passersby on the street, all of them in their jeans or slightly-nicer-than-usual outfits. It's a weekend, so there's not even a cheap suit waiting to grab dinner before heading home after work. Sure there's a few dressed up, we're in New York after all. A few of them are in dresses like Emery's, meaning they're nice, but nothing like the dress I saw on Blythe. Blythe's dress probably cost at least $10,000, and that was before the custom fittings. And I know— because I know my soon-to-be-ex-wife—that she'll never wear it again. I certainly can't imagine her plopping her ass down on a cement planter to eat a gyro. Hell would freeze over before that would happen.

"Mr. Duke," Emery scolds. "Your food's going to get cold. Come *on*."

I sigh and sit down next to her, feeling the rough cement through the fabric of my suit. I watch as Emery continues to inhale her sandwich, attacking it with a ferocity and enthusiasm that, fuck it, completely arouses me. I can't help but imagine her approaching something else with that sort of hunger. I tear my eyes away before my cock gets any ideas about embarrassing me on a sidewalk and dig into the bag for a falafel. I take a bite and find that, damn. It is good. Good and greasy.

"It's better with the white sauce!" Emery interjects with way, way too much excitement about sauce.

White sauce. Fuck my life.

"I'm good," I mutter, trying not to laugh at myself. Fucking ridiculous.

"I told you," Emery says with a satisfied grin. "Now you know why I practically ran over here."

I do laugh, now. "Remind me never to get between you and a falafel, Ms. Mills."

She smiles. "When I'm passionate about something, I go all out. Doesn't matter if it's falafel or…work."

She falters on the last word, turning away with cheeks tinged pink. How was that sentence originally intended to be finished?

She looks at me and then away again, her eyes lighting on the Hilton that's directly across the street from us. Its neon lights blare out over the street, and I imagine that right now Blythe's stewing about why I never arrived at her table. How's she spinning my absence? I decide I don't give a shit. She shouldn't have pulled such a childish move in the first place.

"You really hate her, don't you?" Emery asks.

I meet her gaze. "Am I that obviously thinking about her?"

She shrugs. "We don't have to talk about it if you don't want to. I just… I can see why it would be awkward if we had to sit there with her."

I nod. "Awkward wouldn't begin to describe it."

She doesn't know about Robert and why his presence next to Blythe undoes me so completely. All she knows is that I hate my ex-wife. And because she's just another intern, that's all she needs to know.

"You know, maybe it's not my place, but there's something I think you should know," Emery says, fiddling with the wrapper of her finished sandwich. "About the event tonight."

I arch an eyebrow. "What's that?"

She balls the wrapper up. "Well, it's about the charity."

I sigh. "I knew something was bothering you. Honestly, I wish you'd just spit it out."

Emery purses her lips. "That's easy enough for you to say. You're my boss. You say you're happy to hear my opinion, but do you really mean that?"

"Of course I do," I say. "I want every person who works for me to be honest with me. If they have something to say, they should say it. As long as it isn't a lie, I don't give a shit. It doesn't mean I'll agree with everything they say, but I promise you, Ms. Mills, I can handle it."

She takes a breath and then straightens up.

"Fine," she says. "I think you should know that that charity is garbage and you should be ashamed to be making donations to them."

Well. That wasn't what I was expecting. I'd prepared myself for a personal question about Blythe, maybe even something about my reputation. Not for this.

"You have a problem with a charity for kids?" I say, admittedly incredulous. What could possibly be wrong with a kids' charity?

"That is exactly the reaction that these people want you to have," Emery says. "They want you to see the billboard and the flyers and the website with the cute kids, and they want to tug on your heartstrings so that you don't look any closer. But I looked up the charity while we were there, and do you know they have a D rating on Charity Navigator? That the executives are currently under investigation for skimming so much money that the kids barely get anything?"

"That...that isn't possible," I say, even though I have no idea about anything about this charity. "How would they be able to operate?"

"Because people like you don't do their research," she says, cutting me off before I can defend myself. "Or because they trust people who don't."

She knew I was going to blame Blythe.

"I just think you have an incredible opportunity," she says, sighing. "There are so many charities out there that actually need the money, and they don't have a shot because of charities like this one."

I stare at her. I've never seen her so heated. There's a light in my eyes and a fierce set to her gaze.

"How do you know all of this?" I ask. "You didn't just Google this on a whim."

She fidgets with the balled-up wrapper in her hand, and I watch as she debates whether or not to answer me.

"I'm not mad that you said this," I say, trying to tug an answer out of her. "I meant what I said before. I will always prefer the truth, no matter how much it stings."

This doesn't seem to make her any more willing to explain. In fact, she reddens and looks down. My stomach drops as I worry she might be about to cry, or chicken out on speaking her mind, but then she looks up and her gaze is still fierce, still shining.

"You're right," she says. "It wasn't just a whim. I know a lot about this because of my family. My brother is hard of hearing. There's a charity that worked with us when he was younger since my parents couldn't always afford things for him. His hearing aids, extra classes, speech therapy, all of it, paid for by this charity. He's grown up now, but I don't know what we would have done without them."

She sighs. "And every year, they have to fight for funding. There are no big charity balls for them. No matched donations. And they do such great work. Their executives take a modest salary to run the charity, unlike this one. It's not fair."

I absorb her words, not sure of how to respond. Nothing I can say seems to match what she's just shared with me. I shift awkwardly on the cement.

"I'm sorry," she says. "I don't mean to be harsh. It's just... frustrating to see, that's all. Those kids really need help, and when I think about all the money they're going to lose to inflated overhead, it just pisses me off."

Her passion is breathtaking. Her care and compassion, all of it impresses me. I want to do something that will wipe away her disappointment with tonight, if that's even possible.

"I'll talk to Blythe about the charity," I say. "I don't think we can redirect the funds raised, but maybe we can. But rest assured, it won't happen again."

She looks at me. "I thought you said you don't get involved with the charity side because of her."

"Well, you've reminded me that this is my company," I say. "And besides, if they are as bad as you say, then it's bad for business."

She laughs. "Always the bottom line, Mr. Duke?"

"That's not what I meant," I say.

She shakes her head and stands. "I'm sorry. I don't know what I'm saying. I suppose I just have a lot on my mind."

"Because of the charity? I told you, I'll take care of it."

She shakes her head. "No. Just...thank you for giving me this opportunity tonight, Mr. Duke. I hope I haven't jeopardized it with my big mouth."

Without thinking, I stand up and take her hand. The touch sends a jolt of electricity through both of us. It's different than the heated moment in the copy room, more intimate somehow, and I pull my hand back.

"You haven't ruined anything," I say. "And in fact, I believe that you conducted yourself with exceptional professionalism tonight."

She smiles. "Good. I need this job. Student loans won't pay themselves off, after all."

Student loans. She's a child. A fresh-out-of-college child, my intern. The reminder singes the air between us.

"I'll get you home then," I say.

She nods, and we wait in silence for Leo to arrive. We spend the drive in silence, too, with me running through everything she said and everything I said. Why does it feel like our relationship just got more complicated, when I was the very definition of chaste tonight?

We reach her building. I watch her worry her hands in her lap. At last, she plasters on a smile and turns to me.

"Thank you again, Mr. Duke. See you on Monday."

"Don't forget those notes, Ms. Mills."

She nods, and then she's gone. All I have left is my thoughts, and something tells me they won't be so easy to untangle.

CHAPTER TWELVE

I SPEND the weekend grappling with the fallout of the charity event. Not that there was visible fallout—all media coverage of the event declared it a success and hailed Duke Capital as a "business that gives back to New York"—but my own thoughts can't help replaying every detail of my conversations with Emery.

It's not just that I'm reminded of how her dress hugged every perfect curve of her body, though that's stuck with me, too. Every night, I picture her crawling toward me across the bed, still wearing the dress, begging me to fuck her, telling me she can't wait another second because she needs my hands on her. But it's more than lust. In fact, if anything, our conversation on the sidewalk interrupts the fantasy, because I remember how her lips pouted and how disappointed she looked, not just in Duke Capital, but in me. I had told her I knew everything about my business, and here I was, not only in the dark on something, but misled to a dangerous degree.

She was right about the charity, the one that Blythe selected. It is one step above a scam, and worse, I think, because the people who give money to it genuinely believe they're doing the right thing. Or do they? All it took was a

Google search to find out how terrible they are. Emery is right, people don't pay enough attention to where they donate. Happy to pat themselves on the back and slip the tax write-off to their accountants.

The big question, and the one I can't stop returning to, is whether or not Blythe knows. As much as I hate to admit it, we're a lot alike, business-wise. It seems absurd that she wouldn't know what's going on with the charity. I try to tell myself that maybe she had some executive choose it, that the decision wasn't intentional, but that doesn't line up with the Blythe I know. I know she does a thousand dollar business lunch where she mentions the charity once and writes it off. I know she has that boyfriend of hers do "consulting" work as a way to keep the money cycling between them. But would she go low enough to knowingly have us involved with a charity that is mostly overhead? One that effectively pockets the money meant to help children? I can't say.

Then there's the issue of what to do. Pulling the money feels impossible, but should a charity like this even be in business? My mind is swirling, and as much as I hate it, I know there's only one person who will have any of the answers I need.

I get to the office early on Monday. I need to get this out of the way. My father used to tell me to bite off the "biggest, hairiest" task first thing in the morning. And this is definitely that, given who it involves.

I walk through the empty office and head straight for Blythe's. This used to be a regular walk for me, one I'd take to pick her up for lunch or to meet her at the end of the day. Towards the end, right before things fell apart, it was the last place I'd see her. She'd tell me she needed to stay late, and I'd admire her commitment to the company. She was a perfectionist, I'd tell myself. How lucky I was to have her in my company and my bed.

That was bullshit, obviously. She was staying late for other reasons, but I was too blind and oblivious to see it.

Still, I know her well enough to know that she'll be here early. I walk up to the door and take a breath, knowing I'm about to willingly throw myself into the snake pit. I ready myself to knock, and that's when I hear her girlish giggle.

"Robby," she purrs. "Oh, God, do that again."

My insides go cold, my fingers braced on the doorframe tense. It's bad enough that I've caught her like this before. But here? Nowhere is sacred. Not my home. Not my office.

I could turn around. It'd be easy to walk away. Maybe I could email her, but then, the questions are too sensitive. No, this is something I have to face in person. Besides, I'm not a coward. And if I was going to be a coward, it sure as fuck wouldn't be for her. Especially not for her.

I knock, hard, on the office door. I hear a squeal inside, followed by the shuffling of bodies. I imagine them straightening their jackets and buttoning their pants.

"Just a minute," Blythe calls in a high voice.

She appears a moment later, not a hair out of place. Her cheeks are red, though, and her lipstick's been blotted off a bit. One look at her and we both know I know what she's been doing.

Her eyes narrow and then she smirks. "Harrison. How nice of you to drop by unannounced."

"I need to have a word with you," I say. She's keeping the door open just enough so that I can't see all the way inside. I don't know why she's bothering to hide when we both know who's inside.

"I'm busy at the moment," she says. "Are you finally ready to sign the papers? If so, Claire has them. You can—"

"I'm not here for that," I say. "This is business. Let me in."

She sighs, throwing open the door and turning to head back to her desk. Now, I can see him fully. Straight, dark hair slicked back, sharp blue eyes, taller than most but shorter than me. He's sitting straight in the leather chair in the corner, his legs crossed. He's scrolling through his phone, as if I didn't just catch him—for the second time—screwing my wife on my property. He turns his gaze up to me, and the bastard has the nerve to smile.

"Harrison," he says. "How nice to see you."

"Fuck you," I say.

He rolls his eyes. "How eloquent. Should I let myself out?"

He starts to stand, but I wave for him to stay seated. "No, stay. Since I know you've had your hand in this as well."

"What are you even talking about?" Blythe says, taking a seat at her desk. "Get on with it. I told you, I'm busy."

Her eyes flick to Robert in the seat, both of them smirking. It's bait, but I won't take it.

"It's about the charity from the event on Saturday," I say. "I have some questions."

"Oh, is this about how you bailed during the middle of the event?" Blythe says, clucking her tongue, a smirk slipping across her face. "Even for you, Harrison, that was ridiculously immature. Why couldn't you just sit at the table with us like an adult?"

"I did what I needed to do," I say, keeping my voice firm but steady, even as she's needling me for a reaction. "And this isn't about that. Did you know that that charity's got a D rating? Did you know they only give less than 10% of their donations to the kids? Why the hell did you choose them to support? With my money."

Blythe rolls her eyes. "Now you're just making things up. You know I would never—"

"Blythe, listen to me," I say. "I did the research. I know. What I need to know from you is why. I knew you and the asshole over here were fucking with things, but this? This is just evil."

"Of course you would think I'm evil," she spits back. "You only ever see your bullshit side of any story."

How many times did she scream this at me after I found them together? That I'd been unwilling to hear her out. That I'd driven her to it. And my favorite—that it wasn't what it looked like. She did her best to twist me up in knots with her lies and manipulation and soft grasp on the truth. But it was all bullshit. I knew all I needed to know. She was the one who threw away our marriage and the one who chose my best friend of all people to cheat on me with.

I won't get pulled into her games again. Not today. Not ever.

"This isn't open to interpretation," I say, and spin to Robert. "Did you know about this?"

He turns his phone down and steeples his hands, seemingly considering my question. He blinks his eyes at me like I'm a picture he needs to focus on, and then, after an annoying amount of time, he nods.

"They do good work, Harrison," he says, driving his dagger into my side with his casual use of my name. "I should know. My brother's on their board."

I stare at him. And then I stare at her. For once, she has the decency to look embarrassed, hiding behind her carefully manicured hands.

"Why are you even here?" I question Robert. "Haven't I revoked your building access yet?"

"Oh Harrison, how very territorial of you," Blythe interjects, drawling the words like I'm the unreasonable one in this trio.

"We're pulling out on this one," I say. "I won't be involved with a charity like this."

"So you want to be the corporation that pulls funding from babies, Harrison?" Blythe says. "Can you imagine the PR nightmare? No, things are fragile enough as it is. We keep things the way they are. Besides, they do a lot for the children with the ten percent."

"Do you even hear yourself?" I'm steaming over her casual dismissal of a charity operating with this level of over-head. Overhead that most certainly funds bullshit golf retreats for the board members. "Why? Because I don't want to be associated with anything this shady." It's beneath me, but I give her a measured look when I say it. Shady is as shady does.

She narrows her eyes. "You know it wouldn't just reflect on me, Harrison. Especially since, because of your stubborn-ness, we are still legally married. So I would be careful with your threats."

Rage is building in me. All I can do is glare at her. Just when I thought she couldn't get any lower.

But of course, it's not just her. I turn to look at Robert. He's smirking at me. Years of friendship, and in this moment, he looks at me like something he's trapped in a net. Like besting me is nothing but a game to him.

I remember when I first started having my doubts about Blythe. I knew something was wrong, but I couldn't put my finger on it. It made me irritable at work, colder than usual. Robert suggested drinks, so I could get the stick out of my ass, he'd said. We went to Rose Bar, and he ordered round after round of Manhattans made with the finest whiskey that they kept in stock.

"She's pulling away," I confided in him. "I don't know why."

"Maybe you're working too much," he told me. "You know how women are. Needy."

But Blythe had never been needy. She'd been self-suffi-cient, independent, and headstrong. It had been an incredibly sexy, intoxicating mix. I loved that she and I could be talking business one minute and tearing each other's clothes off the next. So, needy? No, that was never Blythe, and I told Robert that.

"I don't know, man," he said. "Give her some space."

Of course, I had no idea that, while I was with Robert, Blythe was at home, in her finest lingerie, sending him pictures. I had no idea that they were seeing each other later that night. They were already together, and had been for over a month. She'd admit this later in a fight. But in that moment, I knew nothing, and the asshole had the nerve to act like he cared about me. Like the problem with my wife was me rather than an unwelcome third party. Him.

I could tear him apart right now. My best friend. How I ever trusted him is a mystery.

"This isn't over," I promise both of them, and then I pivot and leave the office, slamming the door shut behind me so that the entire frame rattles.

CHAPTER THIRTEEN

I'M STORMING BACK to my office, grateful that it's still early enough that no one is around to witness me gritting my teeth against the anger that's running through me. I knew Blythe and Robert were terrible people. I knew they were willing to fuck over the person closest to them, that being me. But this is on another level. Her scheming isn't just endangering the business, though it's certainly doing that. It's also hurting innocent kids who should be getting help. And there's nothing I can do about it, because she's right. Her PR nightmare would become my PR nightmare. So what the hell do I do?

I stomp back to my own office, where at least I can throw some things if Sandy isn't in yet. I turn a sharp corner intent to cut through a row of cubicles, mumbling to myself about the things I'd like to do to Blythe and Robert when, *smack!*

Even as the familiar burning sensation hits me, right along with the smell of coffee, I can't quite believe it. What are the chances?

But then of course, I look down, and there she is, her lips in an "o" shape and her eyes wide.

"You've got to be kidding me," I say. "Or is this your new

schtick, Ms. Mills? Because I promise you, you don't have to spill your latte on me to start a conversation."

"Shit," she's saying, dropping comically to the ground as she attempts to mop up the mess with a couple of napkins. "Shit, shit, shit."

The corner of my mouth twitches, threatening a laugh. How can someone so innocent looking mutter not just one curse word but four in a row?

"Ms. Mills, please stop," I say. "I'll call maintenance."

Her eyes dart up to mine. I wonder if she's remembering our last mishap. The one with the broken coffee mug that ended with my hands all over her and her wet for me in the break room. Just the thought brings back...feelings. The feel of my hands on her. The feel of her breasts through her blouse. The feel of her flush against me, against the hardness in my pants. From this angle, I can see down her button-down to her breasts, and I avert my eyes. Now isn't the time for a temptation, no matter how delicious it is. I remember the chilly way we ended Saturday, the need for professionalism. I tell myself I was right to attempt to reset this relationship. To resist this—whatever this is.

"I'll have Sandy call maintenance," I say, and step around her to head to my office.

"Wait, Mr. Duke—"

She follows me, clicking after me in her heels. I try to ignore it, to pretend I don't hear her calling after me. It's a childish game, but I grit my teeth and keep pushing forward. I am her boss. There are boundaries. I walk faster, hoping she'll get the message.

"Sandy," I say, not stopping at her desk as I walk briskly past. "Another coffee spill," I deadpan. Call someone to clean it up, please."

Her eyes widen. "Certainly, Mr. Duke. But—"

"I'm just going to change," I say. "I'll be out for my messages in a bit."

I walk straight into my office not waiting on a response. I've got a few changes of clothes in a closet in my office, in case I need a change after a midday workout. Or in case of interns. I grab a fresh shirt and tie and throw them on my desk, wresting my tie off before I start to unbutton my now second ruined shirt. I'm halfway through the buttons when I hear a cleared throat and look up.

In my doorway, Emery stands, worrying her bottom lip as she stares at the bare skin from where I've unbuttoned my shirt. Behind her, Sandy watches curiously.

I sigh, hoping my cool tone will drive her away. "What is it, Ms. Mills?"

Her eyes widen. She looks from Sandy to me. "I...I wanted to apologize for spilling on you. Again. And I wanted to give you my notes from Saturday."

Right. The notes. "It's fine. You can send those in an email to me. Sandy can assist you if you're unfamiliar with the concept."

"I really think it'd be better to go over them in person," she says, ignoring my jibe. "Since it's my first time doing this. I don't want to make any mistakes."

It's such a bullshit excuse, and I glance at Sandy, waiting for her to usher the girl out of my office. She's done it a thousand times with executives who wanted more of my time than I was willing to give.

Instead, Sandy smiles. "I think that's a great idea. In fact, Mr. Duke has time right now; his first meeting isn't until ten. I'll call maintenance about that spill and leave you two to it."

I stare at her. She can't be serious. "Sandy—"

But she's already disappeared and shut the door behind her, leaving Emery and me alone together in my office, with my shirt half undone.

Emery steps toward me. "Why are you avoiding me?"

"I'm not," I say, even though I definitely am. Because my encounter with Blythe this morning has reminded me of another thing. I'm the CEO of the company, and the next appropriate step after divorcing my cheating wife is not a fuck with an intern.

Still, even as the thoughts cross my mind, I lean in and brace my hands against the edge of my desk, because I want to. I most definitely would like a fuck with an intern. With this one, specifically.

"You were ignoring me just now," she says. "I was calling your name, and you kept walking."

Her voice is slightly husky. I straighten, glancing to see her eyes roaming over me, from my chest to my abs. And it's not my stained shirt she's focused on. I know what I look like. I'm a man who takes great pride in my appearance. A man who puts in the necessary work at the gym. I watch her fingers twitch at her side as she moves a step closer. Is she holding back from touching me?

"I haven't been ignoring you," I lie.

"You have," she corrects me, stepping forward a few more steps. Far too many steps because she's close enough to touch me now and she does. Her hand reaching out to touch the damp stain of coffee on my partially unbuttoned shirt, frown lines wrinkling her forehead as she surveys the damage. She's totally matter-of-fact about it while my goddamn dick responds like she's seducing me. "And this ruined shirt isn't my fault. You were the one not watching where you were going. You plowed right into me."

I raise a brow. "Really Ms. Mills? Shifting the blame is beneath you. If you'd been watching where you were going, you'd have been able to avoid me plowing into you."

Terrible choice of words.

"Well either way, you should get this off," she says. Then, God help me, her fingers move to complete the job of unbuttoning my shirt.

I don't stop her. I should. *I should.*

I don't.

When she reaches my waistband she starts matter-of-factly tugging the material free of my pants before she appears to catch herself. A small, "oh," escaping her lips and a blush covering her cheeks as her eyes fly up to mine and then back to my cock.

My cock, which is feeling anything but matter-of-fact about Emery's efforts to rid me of my shirt.

"So you're not entirely impartial to me, then," she murmurs and I nearly laugh. Fucking tease.

She drops her hand, her forehead wrinkled as her eyes drop back to my pants.

"I apologize," I say. "Hazard of a beautiful woman undressing me," I add, taking a step back.

"Wait, though," she interjects, following me that single step. "What if..." she adds, but trails off, the unfinished sentence hanging between us heavier than my cock.

"What if, what?"

"What if I'm not impartial to you either?"

"What are you suggesting, Emery?" I control my breathing and manage to get the words out, which is fairly conscientious for a guy with a hard-on when I think her suggestion was pretty damn clear.

"Well if you're not impartial and I'm not impartial, perhaps I could"—she pauses, and I don't miss that her own breathing is a bit labored—"help you."

"Help me how, exactly?" Jesus Christ she's going to kill me with this conversation.

"I don't know." She shrugs, a small hitch of one shoulder before her eyes fly to mine. "I mean, I know," she adds with meaning, "I'm just not sure I know what you'd like, exactly."

Her offer hangs between us.

I should send her away.

But then she brushes her hand against me and the idea of sending her anywhere is the last thing on my mind. She traces the outline of my cock, already very eagerly straining against the confines of my pants.

"My belt," I say. I should stop her. I should—at the very least—not encourage her. But it's only two words; I'll see what she does with them.

She does not disappoint.

Her motions are quick, jerky as she slides the buckle free and then undoes the button beneath. She follows this with an unsure glance at my face, her breathing unsteady. "We'll need to unzip in order to replace your shirt," she says. "Right?"

Sounds logical.

"Besides, maybe you need some incentive not to ignore me," she adds, sliding the zipper down to my ruin. Because when she's done, she drops to her knees.

Fuck. I should—

Yeah, never mind.

It only takes the slightest tug on my boxer briefs, and my cock is free, fully hard and erect and right in front of her pink lips. She mouths a silent "oh," her brows arched and her head tilted just slightly to the side as she visibly swallows.

I refrain from groaning.

Barely.

She leans in, cupping her hand so softly around my length I think she must be messing with me. Her tongue darts out—only to lick her own lips before retreating.

"Are you trying to give me blue balls, Ms. Mills?" I ask. "Because, if so, you're doing an excellent job."

She startles, as if realizing. "Sorry! I just…you're bigger than I expected. Huge. I wasn't expecting it to be so big."

I audibly groan this time. She's good.

"Definitely not a disappointment," she adds. "I just need to, uh, readjust my, um, plan."

I stare at her. Readjust the plan? Is she fucking kidding? My cock twitches in her palm as she continues to lightly stroke me as if she needs a permission slip to do more, dragging her fingertips slowly from the base to the very tip of me in a featherlight caress.

This might kill me.

I suppose I deserve it.

Yet—

I still want her to grab me, really, truly grab me in that small hand and pump my dick back and forth.

Then she leans forward and, with the tiniest lick, runs her tongue across the crown of my cock.

Fuck.

I can feel my dick swelling with the need to fuck and fuck fast. My cock's aching for release, bordering on pain, and I need to be in her perfect little pink mouth now.

"Do you like that?" she asks from the floor. Another tease of her tongue on my shaft.

"I do," I answer, but even I can hear the incomplete sentence in my tone.

"But what?" She blinks up at me, then adds a soft, "Tell me."

Sweet Jesus.

"Put your mouth on me," I command. "Or Ms. Mills, I swear to God, I'll take care of this problem myself while you watch."

Her brown eyes flick up to me, surprised before a flash of determination appears. She extends that perfect tongue again, sliding it across my shaft in a long wide lick, and I shudder. Cum beads at the crown of my dick, and she tastes it tentatively, swallowing me down.

It's still not enough. I take a step forward so that I'm closer to her face, and then I grab her hair and guide her mouth to my dick with the push of my hand. She opens wide and takes me in, slowly circling her tongue around my head and shaft.

"Lick every inch," I tell her. "Take it all."

She takes the instruction with enthusiasm, rolling her tongue up and down my shaft, letting me guide myself deeper into my mouth. She gags slightly, but adjusts her head so that I touch the back of her throat with my dick. I could come right then but I hold on, intent on making this last as long as possible. She flicks her tongue, her mouth wet and warm and perfect and she pushes me so close to the edge that I know I'm ready to burst.

"Wrap your lips around your teeth," I demand. "And suck. Suck hard, and don't even think about stopping."

She nods and complies, bobbing her head as I push forward, fucking her face as she sucks and flicks her tongue. I grab her hand and guide her to my balls, and the sensations of her fingers against the sensitive flesh makes my toes curl.

I groan as she gets the sense of the motion on her own, no longer needing my guiding to show her the pace. She begins to combine the sucking with the circling of her tongue, pushing me deeper into her mouth. As I strike the back of her throat hard, the orgasm ripples through me like fire, coursing through every inch of me as I spill into her mouth. I shudder with the release, and like a good girl, she keeps her mouth around me, letting my cum drizzle down the back of her throat. Then she swallows with her lips still around me, and I nearly collapse at the intensity of it.

It takes me a moment to catch my breath, and when I do, Emery's there, still on her knees, watching me as I bring my breathing back to normal. She rises, looking at me with those sparkling brown eyes.

"Was that…was that okay?" she asks.

I laugh. "Yes, Ms. Mills. Exemplary effort."

She blushes. "I…I just…"

She bites her lip and glances around. "Perhaps I should let you change your shirt."

I don't know what to say. The shyness has returned to her so suddenly, reminding me like an anvil crashing down around me that she's my intern, my goddamn intern, and I just allowed her—encouraged her—to suck me off in my office.

"We can talk about the notes later," she says. "Or maybe you were right and I'll just go over them with Sandy."

"Ms. Mills, wait—"

"Thank you, Mr. Duke," she says, not really looking at me, and then she turns, clicking her heels out of my office, careful as she opens and shuts my door so that no one can see inside.

Fuck, I think as it shuts, my spent dick still hanging out of my pants. Fuck.

CHAPTER FOURTEEN

WHAT THE HELL have I done?

After Emery leaves my office, I tuck my dick back in my pants and change my shirt. Then I pace, my nerves shot and not just because of my orgasm.

God, that orgasm.

Focus, you dick bag.

That girl is far too sweet for office blowjobs with her boss's boss's boss, without so much as an orgasm in return. Hell, she's probably never even kissed a guy that didn't take her to dinner first. She probably lost her virginity to her prom date a full six months after he told her he loved her. And then he likely spent the rest of the summer bringing her flowers and buying her Dairy Queen or whatever the fuck they do in Kansas to woo a girl.

Fuck that guy. Jesus Christ, I need to focus.

Because what did I just do? Fucked her face in my office. Used her and threw her out afterwards. I didn't even give her an orgasm first. Or after. Zero orgasms for her. I bet all she's thinking about is, *wow, what a goddamn asshole.*

Which she already thought, didn't she? Harrison Duke, the cold CEO who's obsessed with his business and doesn't even know or care what's going on with his own charity department. A guy old enough to be her, admittedly, young father. But still.

Really young father. Like still in high school.

Fuck.

This is unacceptable. I glance at the stack of work on my desk, contracts that need to be dealt with. There's a sticky note from Sandy reminding me about a call with Pink after lunch. I'm glad we're pushing forward, and I'm even more glad that Monica's pushing to be paid fairly. I don't mind playing hardball with someone who knows their business is worth it.

This is what I should be focused on. Work. Not some bumbling girl straight out of a romcom who spills coffee on me and sucks my dick like she was born to please me. *Work.* And I don't need to have a shred of guilt about this, do I? She's a consenting adult. It's not a crime to get off on a bumbling midwestern blowjob. She dropped to her knees and grabbed my dick, I didn't ask her to. She could've left my office any time.

But the guilt doesn't go away, even as I finally stop pacing and sit, dashing off a few emails and making a few calls. I'm able to put it to the side of my mind, but it sits there, pulsing like a headache. Building. Gnawing. This won't go away unless I deal with it.

The question is, *how* do I deal with it?

I eat lunch in my office, keeping the door shut, even to Sandy. I handle the rest of the day's business, including the call with Pink. I'm decisive, straightforward. I pour everything into work. I do this until there isn't any work left, and still, the guilt pierces me.

Fine, I decide. I'll take her to dinner. Dessert and after-dinner drinks. Maybe I'll give her an orgasm in the back of the car on the way home. Privacy partition up, of course. Dinner and an orgasm for her, the two things lacking from this morning, plus something sweet. Then, we'll be even. This heated attraction will be something for both of us to tuck away as a fond memory, with our lust equally abated.

Except, this idea presents a new problem. Where to take her? I've been to every must-dine restaurant in the city with my witch of a wife. My soon to be ex-wife. Which shouldn't matter. I shouldn't allow Blythe to ruin the best things about this city. And I won't. But will I be able to focus on giving Emery the attention she deserves with the memories of Blythe breathing down my neck?

Doubtful.

Though if I'm being truthful I know I could focus on Emery in the midst of a hurricane. Yet I still don't want to take her anywhere old. I want to try something new with her.

A new restaurant. That's it.

Besides it's doubtful if Emery would even like any of my usual restaurants. I remember the way she devoured the falafel gyro at the food cart on Saturday. Maybe there's a Middle Eastern restaurant somewhere in this city that would be a good fit. I devote far more time than I'd like to admit to research, even requesting that Leo investigate a few of the options for me. After he reports back, I decide on one, an upscale restaurant that is said to serve the finest falafel in the state. We'll see if it's a match for Emery's beloved food cart.

I book the reservation, and that's it, I've accomplished everything I need for the day. Except, I realize, for Emery herself. I need to actually ask her to join me.

I have her number from the event. Sandy gave it to me in case I needed to call her, but since I didn't, it's never been used. I punch her number into a text and tell myself I'm making things right, ending things rather than starting them.

I draft a message.

Harrison: **Would you like to join me for dinner tonight? Middle Eastern food. 8 p.m. I'll pick you up.**

I debate the phrasing. Do I mention business to make sure she understands? But then, today wasn't business, no matter how much I tried. Not that I tried that hard. For some reason, all my good intentions fall apart around this girl. But the point stands that today was clearly pleasure, and that pleasure needs to be reciprocated. I leave the message as is and fire it off.

I'm prepared to spend however long it takes staring at my phone, waiting for her to reply like some kid waiting for his high school crush to text him back, when a knock at the door saves me from my own ridiculousness. I look up just as Ramon cracks the door open.

"Hey boss," he says. "Just wanted to check in."

I glance at him, momentarily suspicious. Robert used to like to "check in," but it was usually his way of fishing for something, time off or a favor or something similar. But then I remind myself, again, that Ramon isn't like that. This might be a friend who actually cares about me, no matter how difficult that is to comprehend.

"Can't complain," I say, thinking somewhat guiltily about the fact that, hours ago, Emery was in this very office with my cock in her mouth, sucking me off like it was a part of her job description.

I look over at my phone, turned facedown on my desk. I'm tempted to check it for a reply from Emery, but I resist. I'm a grown man having a conversation with a business associate. I need to act like it.

"I heard there was a bit of an argument between you and Blythe in her office this morning," Ramon says, cutting right to the point. "And I just wondered if you wanted to talk about it."

I can't help but snort. "You heard?"

"You know people talk."

"Indeed," I muse. "But I'm not sure how you can help. Unless you can come up with a viable reason I can use to fire my ex-wife. Also, when did we escalate this friendship to the discussion of our feelings? Shouldn't we have had a sleepover first? Exchanged friendship bracelets? Something?"

Ramon shifts a bit, almost as if he's reconsidering if he should have come into my office in the first place. But then he strides forward and takes a seat across from me and knits his hands together on the desk.

"Isn't that part of the problem, Harrison?" he asks, clearly ignoring my attempts to derail the conversation by behaving like a dick. "She isn't your ex-wife. You're still married."

I bristle. I've already dealt with this from Blythe this morning. I don't need it from a friend, particularly one that I was just starting to admit that I liked.

"Hear me out," he says, clearly reading my annoyed expression. "I'm worried that you're making choices that aren't the best for you. Refusing to divorce Blythe. Interns…"

My heart stops for a second before I remember that he's referring to walking in on Emery and me in the break room, not the blowjob she gave me in my office earlier today. I give him what I hope is a dismissive, conversation-ending look. "One intern, not interns. And it was nothing."

The blowjob was definitely something, but I keep that to myself.

"I'm sure it was," he says. "But it's not like you. You've always been the kind of man that didn't stoop to levels like that."

"You'll have to keep telling me what kind of man I am," I say, colder than I mean to. I'm not angry at Ramon. I'm disgusted with myself. "I wasn't aware that you had such a pure opinion of me."

"I'm not saying that you can't have fun," he says. "But you built this business from the ground up. Don't you want to protect it?"

I hate that, the more he says, the more annoyed I get. Not because he's wrong, though. It's because he's right. I know that I'm crossing a thousand different lines by entertaining even the idea of something with Emery. But I remind myself that I've done what I can to make that right, haven't I? I'm going to level the field with dinner, and then I'm going to step aside.

Not that Ramon needs to know any of that.

"I'm as protective of my business as anyone would be," I say evasively. "Though, as always, I appreciate your honesty."

He sighs, knowing that he's lost the battle, whatever it was about. He starts to stand, but stops.

"Maybe I'm overstepping," he adds. "But I just want you to know that you deserve to be happy. You'll move on and find someone, you know. Someone special. Your forever doesn't end with Blythe."

My insides are ice at those words. How could Ramon possibly understand what it's like to have your entire life ripped out from under you? What would his reaction be, I wonder, if he walked into his home and found his best friend's face buried between the legs of his wife? Would he be able to find something "special" again?

Not that it matters. I've decided that love isn't in the cards for me, and after being married to Blythe, I'm fairly sure it never existed in the first place, anyway.

"Thank you," I tell him, keeping my voice as flat as possible. "I'll remember that."

He nods, clearly wondering if he should say something else. Thankfully, he decides against it.

"Have a good rest of your day," he tells me. "And remember, I'm here if you need me."

Then, he's out of my office and clicking the door shut. And like that same eager schoolboy who's just faced a lecture he has no interest in listening to, I immediately flip over my phone.

Emery: **Can't wait. See you then.**

She ends with an emoji, another reminder of how young she is. But I don't care. Damn it to hell, and damn Ramon's warnings, too.

I've made my bed.

And now it's time to lie in it one last time.

CHAPTER FIFTEEN

THIS TIME, I do not make the mistake of going to Emery's door to pick her up. Chivalry be damned. I can't take the risk of a repeat of what happened today in my office. So, even though Leo gives me a disappointed glare, I text Emery from the car when we're almost there. As we drive up, I spot her standing on the sidewalk, wearing a flowing skirt and nearly sheer top. She's pulled on a long white coat and has her hair done up again. She looks so delicate, like a flower waiting to be plucked.

I do get out to open the door for her, and she smiles at me, batting her long lashes as she does.

"Thank you, Mr. Duke," she says. "How gentlemanly of you."

Feeling guilty, I say, "I should have come to the door."

She waves her hand. "It's okay. My roommates were there. They're playing drunk-strip-Pictionary."

I raise an eyebrow. "That's a thing?"

She laughs. "Absolutely. Probably best that my boss didn't see them all in their underwear."

"I take it you weren't playing?"

A mischievous smile crosses her face. "Why, Mr. Duke. Of

course I was. I was wearing much more before. Thank goodness you got here when you did, or I'd be naked for our date."

"This isn't a date," I say automatically, skipping over the word *naked* entirely. "I just wanted a chance to repay you for earlier."

She looks surprised, and maybe a little hurt? She attempts to school her expression into something a bit more neutral before she responds. A quick blink and a small shake of her head. "You're taking me to dinner because of…earlier?"

I feel myself getting twisted into a knot. I have to stop this before it goes further.

"After you," I say, ignoring her question and gesturing to the still-open car door.

She looks like she wants to say more, but in the end, she slides into the car. As she does, her skirt rides up a bit, exposing the top of her thigh. My pants tighten at the sight.

"Good evening, Ms. Mills," Leo says from the front. "It's good to see you again."

I roll my eyes at Leo's politeness. I know he thinks he's on to something here. Trying to make more of this than it is. He was beside himself earlier when I said we were driving to the same address as Saturday.

"Good evening," Emery says, cutting me a smile and a wink as she slides across the back seat to make room for me. "And likewise."

Leo glances at me in the rearview, giving me a clear "I like this one" look. I give him one that tells him that he better get moving before I have to say something. Thankfully, after our years together, he just smiles and pulls away from the curb.

"So," I say as Leo puts up the partition. "This place. It's supposed to be good."

"I'm excited," she says. "I've only been to a few places since I moved here. That place we went for lunch was probably the nicest."

"The nicest, but not quite as good as your food cart?" I ask.

She laughs. "What can I say? I'm a cheap date."

"Not tonight," I say. "Tonight, you're an expensive date."

As soon as the words are out of my mouth, I realize they sound filthy. I'd meant it to mean that I plan on treating her, but it came out like I'm taking out a prostitute, not my innocent intern.

"Oh?" Emery says. "Am I?"

She turns in her seat to look directly at me and somehow slides closer all in one move. Immediately, blood rushes to my dick in eager anticipation. It remembers her mouth and the swirl of her tongue, and I'd bet there's already a bit of pre-cum at the tip.

Fuck. Why does she do this to me?

Emery places a hand on my leg, just above my knee. Not nearly close enough to cause any real effect, if seduction is what she's going for.

Hoping that's what she's going for, I place my hand over hers and slide it higher.

She smiles and blushes at the same time, pulling her bottom lip between her teeth as if she's trying to control the smile. As if she suspects her cheeky grin isn't the ideal of sexy.

It wouldn't normally be, but on her it's enchanting.

Her eyes dart away from mine and back again, her tongue sweeping her bottom lip as her fingertips begin to explore, tiny circles as she trails closer to my bulge. She gets closer and closer to where I want her with her circling, the touch soft yet deliberate, evidence she's learned from earlier. I lean against her, and slip one hand under her thigh, urging her to straddle me. Her eyes widen for a moment, before she understands what I want and swings her leg over, her skirt riding all the way up to her hips. Through my pants, I feel the thin fabric of her panties, the heat of her as she grinds against my cock.

"Mr. Duke," she whispers, leaning over to say the word against my ear, or perhaps she's lacking the courage to say it to my face. "I think you missed me," she flexes her hips as she says it, making it clear exactly which part of me missed her.

"I warned you once," I say. "You're playing with fire."

I nip at her neck, and she lets out a delicious little moan. I reach up and tease her nipples through her shirt, finding that the fabric of her bra is as thin as paper. It might as well not be there at all.

"Yes," she murmurs. "Wow, that feels so good. I love it when your hands are on me."

God, I could have her right here. I could—

"Five minutes, Mr. Duke and Ms. Mills," Leo announces via the intercom, reminding me that, one, we aren't alone, and two, we have dinner plans.

Emery pulls back a bit, her hips still firmly locked against mine. Her lips hovering just inches from my own. It's weirdly intimate, the almost kiss. This close, I can count every single freckle on her nose. Her lips are parted, and the excitement shining in her eyes is clear.

"I guess we'll have to wait," she says.

"I guess so," I say.

She slides off of me after that, returning to her side of the car. Unlike before, the sights of New York don't hold her attention. Instead, she continues to watch me, and I'd bet money that she's undressing me in her mind. I certainly am. In fact, I'm imagining pushing her back against these seats and tearing off those dainty little panties with my teeth, testing how wet her pussy is for me with my tongue.

"We're here," Leo says, and thank God. I need to get out of this car. I do my best to tamp down my erection before I step out and hold the door open for Emery, who casts another smile up at me.

"I'm starving," she says.

"Well, let's hope it stands up to your high falafel standard," I say.

She smirks. "We'll see."

We walk into the restaurant, which is filled with rich marble flooring and wood paneling. A waiter guides us to our private table, and though this one doesn't have quite the view of Charlie Bird, it does look out onto the street. The smell in the restaurant is impressive, filled with rich spices. A plate of hummus and pita is brought out, and Emery immediately grabs a slice and dips it generously in the hummus. When she bites into it, she lets out a noise of satisfaction.

"Oh," she says. "That's good. That's dang good."

"Dang?" I grin at her use of expletive, barely a swear at all. I want to remind her that it's just hummus, just bread, but she treats everything with the enthusiasm of someone who expects today to be their last. I'm both charmed and curious. What brought out this attitude? Is it just living in Kansas? Maybe living there makes every day feel the same. I don't know. I've only ever known New York where every day feels like a fucking sprint.

"Dang…" She grins, amused with herself. "I prefer to swear with ladylike grace."

I take a bite myself. She's not wrong, it's dang good. As is her company. Have I ever enjoyed myself like this on a date before? *Except it's not a date*, I remind myself. *Just a quick quid quo pro. That's it.*

"Mr. Duke," Emery says, drawing me back to her. "I wanted to ask you a question, if it's all right."

I flinch. I know what she's going to ask. Why haven't I done anything about the damn charity problem? I'm about to tell her I'm working on it, but she cuts me off.

"It's about the man that was at the table with Ms. Lawrence-Duke at the charity event," she says. "I mean, the man with your, um, wife."

My insides tighten. I hate that anyone knows about the

two of them, but of course, they do. The longer I drag out the divorce, the more brazen Blythe becomes. Even if she isn't open about the relationship, people pick things up. Like with her stunt at the charity event table. And as Ramon has pointed out, people talk. If it gets out, she'll blame me for not divorcing her more quickly.

"What about him?" I ask, colder than I intend.

"I just… Who is he? I saw him leaving the office today, and I remembered seeing him on Saturday," she says. "And I just…"

She trails off. I don't blame her. How do you ask this question? Is this the man your wife's fucking? It's not an easy sentence to get out.

"His name's Robert," I say. "I've known him since before I started Duke Capital. We were friends. Best friends, actually."

She leans forward on her elbows, fully immersed in what I'm saying. Blythe was always too reserved to show such enthusiasm. Her attention was often on her phone, or in scanning the room for someone she knew. I took it as a sign of devotion, because it was always Duke Capital she claimed to be working on. But to have this, someone paying attention, drinking in your every word, it's…nice.

"We came up together," I say. "He would give me business advice. He works in an adjacent field, and we could understand each other. I felt like I could trust him. Until, of course, I couldn't."

The image returns to me, as it always does, of him and Blythe. Her lipstick smeared across his face. Her hands clutching his back. Him hovering above her, on my couch.

"I found them together," I say. "Robert and Blythe. Sleeping together. Apparently, the affair had been going on for months."

It feels strange to say the words out loud. I've never told anyone, not even my divorce attorney. I have no idea what Blythe's told Claire. She has her own divorce attorney, obviously. But she has plenty of access to Claire around the office and I don't doubt she's dropped her own version of events whenever possible. Did she mention the infidelity, being caught literally in the act? Or did she leave that bit out to save face? Spin it as they fell in love later?

It doesn't matter.

"You make a vow," I say, the words coming out faster now. "You say you'll love each other forever. But then you find out it's all a lie. That everything, even the foundation, is rotten? You signed up for one thing, and you got something else. Something terrible."

I look up and Emery's eyes are wide and shining.

"Your parents divorced, right?" I ask, and she nods. "See, just another example. And the anger... God, I can't even begin to describe it. Every day that I have to see her, it takes everything in me not to scream at her in front of everyone. That she's not the innocent party, she's the devil. Even though I know for a fact that she's saying the same thing about me behind closed doors."

"But you aren't the devil," Emery says quietly.

"No," I say. "But that doesn't matter. Hell, I'm sure people view me as the heartless asshole who kicked her out of the apartment. I'm the one stalling on the divorce. But I can't explain it. I just... She took so much from me. She caught me off guard, which I detest. And I can't give her another win."

I know I've said too much, and I'm dumping it on someone who shouldn't have to deal with the baggage of a guy like me. To a girl who's splitting an apartment with two other people, just starting out and trying to make it. I'm the one who's so wrapped up in his own world that I don't even notice the problems right under my nose. And yet here I am, dropping it all at the feet of this girl. This impossibly beautiful girl who's watching and listening as if I'm a person worth her time. As if everything I say is of importance and interest to her.

I don't deserve her attention. I should leave now, but I don't. It wouldn't even be possible, not as long as she's looking at me like that.

"Mr. Duke, I had no idea," she says. "Truly."

"Well, there it is," I say. "I'm an old bastard and a cuckold."

Emery smiles, reaching across the table to take my hand. "You're not old, and you're only a little bit of a bastard. Which, I'd like to say, is growing on me."

Her thumb rubs a small circle on my palm. I swallow hard, remembering her body against mine in the car. It doesn't matter how she touches me. I just want more of her, more, more, more. With her, I'm greedy, willing to take everything she has. Didn't I come here with the plan to make this about her? To give her dinner and an orgasm? And yet, instead, I drop the burdensome details of my pending divorce.

"Well, that was heavy," I say. "We should lighten this up. Why don't we figure out what we want to order?"

She picks up the menu, considering it.

"I have to say, I'm feeling pretty full from the hummus," she says, raising an eyebrow. "What would you say about skipping straight to dessert?"

"But what about the falafel?" I ask. I did pick this restaurant out with a particular purpose in mind.

"Mr. Duke," she says, lowering her voice. "What if I told you I was feeling rather…distracted." Those words could be taken a variety of ways. But the way in which she says them, with a swipe of her tongue across her lower lip and a blush hinting across her cheeks…my cock gets the message loud and clear.

"I'd say that dessert sounds like a great idea." I'd also say she should be calling me Harrison by now, but all this Mr. Duke shit is turning me on more than I care to admit.

We order a pudding to share between us, and I watch as

she licks the spoon between each bite, dragging her tongue slowly against the metal. I remember her choking on my dick, and why the fuck are we still in this restaurant?

"Waiter," I say, throwing my card at him as he hustles over. "Go ahead and run that. And quickly, please."

"But I'm not finished," she teases, knowing exactly what she's doing to me.

"Don't worry," I say. "I'll take care of finishing you."

CHAPTER SIXTEEN

WE MANAGE to make it to my apartment fully clothed, but it's a close call. As soon as we're inside the elevator I've got her pressed against the side. She moans as I grind against her, maneuvering one of her legs around my hip so I can press her fully to me. Her mouth meets mine in a frenzy, lips bruised as we each beg for more and more and more. I drag my lips from hers to kiss along her jaw and her neck, and her hands fumble at my belt and the buttons of my pants until she can reach inside to grab hold of my cock.

"Like this?" she questions in a whisper against my ear. We're alone in the elevator and my cock is already in her hand so the whispering seems unnecessary, but so very Emery. She must remember what I taught her yesterday, because her motions are just the right amount of rough as she works her hand over my shaft. I groan, leaning deeper into her hand as she pumps me up and down.

"Not too much," I tell her. "I have other plans."

She nods, and then we're kissing again, our tongues gliding over each other, desperate for more. I let my own hand slip down her chest, cupping her breast and squeezing until she sighs against me.

"Yes," she begs. "Please."

The elevator dings, opening on my floor. I block the doors from closing as she moves to drag me out of the elevator, grabbing her arm and spinning her back to me, staring down into those doe eyes as I force myself to breathe.

"You understand what's about to happen right? If we get off this elevator, and we go inside my place, I'm going to fuck you senseless," I tell her. "Tell me that's what you want."

Her breath catches and her eyes widen at my bluntness, but she nods. Her face is flushed and she tugs on my hand, encouraging me to move this conversation from the elevator to my apartment.

"Yes," she says softly, practically melting against me. "Let's do that."

Then we're stumbling through my front door, drunk on sexual tension and the promise of what's to come. I tug her behind me, hand tucked in mine, headed straight for the stairs. If I had an ounce of composure left in me, I'd drag this out. Stop and offer her a drink. Make use of the terrace I paid so dearly to get. Slide my hand slowly underneath her skirt as she enjoyed the view and squealed about the possibility of someone seeing us.

Fuck composure, I do none of those things. *Next time*, I tell myself. *I'll seduce her with hours of foreplay next time.*

"Wow," she says, her steps faltering. "You live here? By yourself?"

"Yes," I tell her, spinning her into my arms, nipping at her neck with my teeth. "I can give you a tour later."

She laughs, no doubt recalling her offer to give me the tour of her own apartment. Of her bedroom. The tour I refused because I was hell-bent on stopping whatever is happening between us. Now, of course, I know that stopping this is impossible. She is a magnet, the fucking sun, yanking me closer and compelling me to worship her. I could live a hundred lifetimes and not have enough time to do all the things I want to do to her. To show her all the pleasure I want to lavish on her. To give each inch of her body the attention it deserves. But tonight, at least, I can start. I can show her just how much I want her, and I won't rest until she's limp with satisfaction, until she can't even hear the word *orgasm* without thinking of me. Much less have one.

"You have stairs?" Her footsteps come to a full stop now, her eyes widening as she glances around her once again as if to verify we're inside my apartment and not passing through another lobby.

"And a bedroom," I urge her in front of me so I can follow her up the stairs. I can't very well tug her up behind me in those heels. I have some etiquette. A smidge.

When we reach the top of the stairs I lift her so that she's straddling me, carrying her the remainder of the way to the bedroom as she wiggles herself against me and runs her lips along the side of my neck.

Then, finally, I'm laying her on the bed, staring down at her as she stretches luxuriously against the sheets. Wondering why I ever thought this isn't exactly where she belonged.

What were my objections again? I have no idea. Surely they were irrelevant. And likely stupid.

"A little bigger than mine," she says, blinking her eyelashes at me. She clutches a handful of the bedding in her fist, her eyes flickering to my waistband before returning to mine, a hint of apprehension crossing her face even as she lightly arches her back and inches her legs open.

I grin, recalling her referring to my cock as bigger than she expected.

"I'm sorry I refused to go into your bedroom that night," I admit. "I was a stupid, stupid man."

"I wanted you," she tells me. "But then, I want you every time I see you. I get all hot and achy and curious if you're feeling the same. Secretly wishing you'd just grab me kiss me and"—she pauses and swallows, eyeing me from head to toe

—"other things. The very first time I ran into you, when I spilled coffee all over you. I felt it even then."

The vulnerability, the honesty both work to unravel me. Because I feel the same way, even if I can't tell her that.

"Come here," she whispers.

I kneel on the bed and she fists my shirt, pulling me down to her, our lips crashing, our greed equal. I run my hand down her cheek, her neck, and then to her breasts. Such perfect tits, I think, as I bend down and pull one of her hard-as-diamonds nipples into my mouth through the fabric, sucking hard.

She moans, arching her back into the bed, fisting her hands in the sheets.

"These tits," I tell her. "Perfect. You're perfect."

She pants in response as I trail a lazy circle around her nipple, before palming the weight of her in my hand, relishing in the firmness of her flesh. As she arches again, they bounce before me, each nipple hard and swollen.

"Too many clothes," she gasps. "Off. Now."

"Impatient," I tease, but I let her sit up and tug off her blouse. There's that useless bra that I was expecting, so thin and lacy that it might as well not exist at all. Still, I don't want to rush her into taking it off, so I slowly trail the curve of lace with my fingertip, before tugging it down and swirling my tongue around her nipple as she moans.

"Please," she begs. "I can't—"

I'm not immune to begging so I undo the clasp and yank the ridiculous scrap off her body, and there they are before me, each breast a perfect mound, peaked with dusky pink nipples. Her skin is impossibly soft as I suck a nipple between my lips, biting her softly between my teeth, my cock aching with the need to be inside her now. But that need will have to wait until I've explored every inch of her. I want to know exactly what makes her moan. I want to research every curve and catalog her responses to every caress, lick, or pinch I can administer. Because now that she's here, in my bed, every-thing else has fallen away, leaving only us and this all-encom-passing need that needs to be sated.

I kiss my way down her body, enjoying how her hips buck against me when I reach her stomach. My God. I can only imagine how wet she must be, and I decide I need to know. With my left hand, I run a finger up one leg, under her skirt until I reach her sweet pussy. I tease her through her panties —damp—feeling the swollen lips, toying with her, rubbing circles around her clit through the fabric.

Enough of the panties.

She's eager to help me, pushing her panties down when I begin to ease them over her hips, until that perfect, gorgeous pussy is on display just for me.

I slide a finger inside of her, relishing how her hot flesh clenches against me immediately. She cries out, her fingertips tightening on my back.

My God. She's so tight. So fucking tight.

She grinds against my hand, and I work the nerves of her clit with my thumb as I pump deeper and deeper inside of her. Her pussy grows wetter with every thrust of my finger, adjusting to the pressure, clamping down on me and making my cock swell as I imagine replacing my finger with my dick. When I glance at her face, her eyes are shut tight, her mouth open in shock as if this is a novelty. I smile to myself. Yes, I'm going to blow her mind tonight.

I lean in and kiss the spot where her neck meets her shoulder and thrust in deeper with my finger. She moans and pants, bucking hard as I slide in and out of her. She's so tight that I nearly pause at adding a second finger. But she's so wet, so ready for me, that I press forward. Her flesh yielding to accept the invasion. Murmurs of "oh God, oh God," falling from her lips. Oh God is right. Because God help me, I have to be inside her soon or I'll explode.

I pull my fingers out but continue to play with her clit, the bunched up skirt around her waist the only piece of her clothing that remains. Her legs part, and I kiss the inside of her thigh. Then the other. Then tease my tongue across her clit. Just a hint. A quick taste. She's perfect, as sweet as I expected, and she shivers at even this small contact with my tongue, a low moan emerging from her throat and her hips nearly bucking me off of her.

I sit up. She looks up at me, her breasts heaving. Her gaze lands on me and she reaches up to tug on my shirt.

"We're not even," she says, trying to yank it over my head. "In the name of equality, I demand that you remove this shirt."

I smirk. "Well, if it's in the name of equality."

I unbutton, slowly undoing one button after the other, watching her take me in me with those big doe eyes. Finally at the last one, I shrug the shirt off, and she leans forward, running her fingers down the planes of my abs.

"Mr. Duke," she purrs. "These are some very impressive muscles you have here."

"Well, you should know," I say. "You've spent enough time spilling coffee on me the past few weeks."

She smiles. "It was only twice. And it wasn't like it was on purpose."

I lean down and kiss her jawbone. "Are you sure?"

"Yes," she shivers at the touch. "And I'm still blaming the second time on you."

I grin, standing to get my pants off. My cock strains against the thin fabric of my boxer briefs, standing at clear attention for Emery to see. She reaches out greedily, pulling them down until my cock springs into full view, a bead of cum appearing on the tip as she wraps her hand around me.

"It's even bigger than I remembered," she says, running her tightened fist up and down the length. I shudder at the sensation of her hand on me, hypersensitive at her touch.

She leans forward and licks the cum from the tip, and I

hiss, thrusting against her lips and across her tongue. I want to feel her around me again, and thankfully, she's on the same page because she wraps her beautiful lips around the tip, circling her tongue around until it's slick. Then, she pushes forward, taking as much as she can and sucking greedily as she bobs forward and back. The sensation is so strong, I grab the nightstand and hold it as she works her way over my dick, moaning as I strike the back of her throat with one of my thrusts.

She pulls back and licks her lips, but then she's moving down, pulling my balls into her mouth, sucking each one with gentle, then hard motions. She works the shaft with her left hand as she does, then flicks her tongue curiously along the nerves at the base of my cock. Fuck, she's exploring it, working her way over the entire thing with her tongue. I'll never last like this, and I don't want to come in her mouth. Not this time, when there's another option on the table.

"Stop," I say. She looks up at me, my cock still in her hand, her fist still moving over the length. The sight is—

Focus, I remind myself.

"I don't want to come," I say. "Not yet."

"No?" she asks, a teasing glint to her eye.

"No," I say.

I reach over to the nightstand and pull out a condom. I'm unwrapping it when I glance over and see that Emery's shifted slightly on the bed, tensing her shoulders as she bites her lip. It's not the sexy way she did earlier tonight. It's the way she did when she had something to tell me, but she thought I didn't want to hear it.

Her eyes flick away when she sees me watching her. She looks down, clearly bashful, and her legs even pull a bit closer together. The action confuses me. After all, what could have changed between her straddling me in the elevator and now?

She fidgets again, then seems to realize she's still got her skirt on, hiked up around her hips. She unzips and slides it off, but her hands shake, her movements nervous as opposed to seductive.

Suddenly, little details start to add up in my mind. The fumbly-at-first blowjob. The need for reassurance on her technique. The sweet blushes and at the moment—the tenseness in her shoulders and her inability to meet my gaze.

Exactly how experienced is she?

CHAPTER SEVENTEEN

I TRY to gauge what I'm dealing with here. She's far too old to be a virgin, thank Christ. But maybe she hasn't been with very many men. Or perhaps the sex wasn't great?

And surely she's never fucked her boss before, so there's that added to the mix.

Most importantly, how in the hell am I supposed to ask her without insulting her?

I tap the condom package against my fingertips. I remember the blowjob the other day—her tentative motions, her glances at me, looking for reassurance. At the time I'd thought it was the whole boss thing, but perhaps it was inexperience. Or uncertainty about being rejected. Just now, the way her lips and tongue were working my cock, sucking my balls, no uncertainty there. She's confident once she's sure she's not going to be rejected.

Maybe she was speaking from experience when she said she liked the Pink proposal? She'd said something about some women watching porn to learn techniques. Some asshole in Kansas probably told her she was a terrible lay. Or didn't make it good for her. Or pushed her into something she didn't want. The last thought makes my blood boil. Whatever the reason, I'm almost positive that I need to slow this down. After all, she wasn't tense until I reached for the condom. And if she needs me to slow down, no matter how much my cock is aching to drive into her, I'll do it.

I toss the condom back on the nightstand and watch as her eyes follow it.

"I changed my mind," I say. "There's something I want to do first."

She perks up at that. "Oh?"

Fuck, the look in her eyes. Pure trust. Trust that I'll give her exactly what she desires, that I'll make this good, and I intend to be worthy of that look on her face.

"I need another taste of you," I tell her. "Besides, I promised you something to make up for cutting dessert short, didn't I?"

"Something better?" she asks, her voice a tease. She's biting her lip to keep from smiling, her confidence back. But she's blushing nearly everywhere and she's just twisted her ankles together.

"Something much, much better," I promise, uncrossing her ankles and sliding her across the sheets until her ass is at the edge, legs bent open before me.

She yelps.

I kneel at the edge, and before she can say a word, I flatten my tongue against her clit. Much more than a flick this time.

The sound she makes would be enough to make me hard, if I wasn't already. A guttural, hungry moan, followed by a bit of a squeal as her legs tighten around my head and an assortment of incoherent words fall from her lips. I keep going, sucking her clit, circling her entrance with my tongue, relishing in the taste of her and how her hand tightens in my hair, her legs relaxing again as she realizes I have no plans to make this quick. I could devour her all night, eat her out for eternity, if that's what it takes to give her an orgasm she'll never forget. An orgasm she deserves. I work her with wide swipes of my tongue, suck her clit between my lips, rim her entrance with my fingertip, teasing inside until she's begging for release. Nearly shaking with need, so sensitive and ready to explode.

I slip my tongue inside her again and then I focus on her clit, knowing she's ready to burst. Sucking it between my lips, nipping lightly with my teeth, then flattening my tongue against her in long sweeps until she shatters. Her body arches, one hand fisting in my hair, the other grabbing a handful of sheet, as she screams out in pleasure.

"Harrison," she breathes my name out, and it's so pure on her lips. Like a goddamn prayer. I keep my mouth on her until I know I've wrung every last ounce out of this orgasm. Until she's done, her entire body shivering as she comes down.

But my name. I need to hear her say it again. And again. I slide a single finger into her. She's so tight from her orgasm, wet from the same. So perfectly wet and slick. Fuck me, I can't wait to be inside of her. But first things first. Or second things second, as it were. Because I coax another one out of her, playing her with my fingers, toying with, rimming her entrance until she's incoherent, then clamping around my finger so tightly my cock twitches in greed. When she's done, I slide my finger out of her and into my mouth before laying down beside her. Propped on one elbow so I can look at her, I rest my other hand on her lower stomach because I can't not be touching her. My thumb brushes back and forth, smoothing small circles on her skin while I wait for her to speak.

"Harrison," she whispers. "That was...I don't even have words for what that was."

It's my name on her lips that undoes me. I want to hear it again as I fuck her, but that won't happen without some clarification. Yes, she said she wanted this, but I don't want to push her into anything.

"Emery," I say, running my hand along her cheek until she opens her eyes to look at me. "Is there something, uh, you need to tell me?"

"Yes." She blinks at me, her gaze a mixture of satisfaction and rekindling desire. "I want the rest."

"The rest?" I grin, arching a brow at her sassy answer, despite my desire to get some answers.

"All of it," she wraps her hand around my cock and pumps and I nearly lose my focus. I place a hand over hers, stilling her movements. Because God help me, if this conversation lasts much longer I'll be coming in her hand.

"That's not what I meant," I nudge.

Her lips part, her tongue darting out to wet the lower. "I don't have any STDs," she finally says. "Is that what you mean?"

"Nice to know, and same. But not what I was getting at."

She stares at me, silent. Her cheeks still flushed from her orgasm, her eyelashes fluttering against her cheek as she waits for me to elaborate. I stare at her, wondering how best to broach this. My cock throbs in her hand and there's no mistaking the want in her eyes. But there's also no mistaking the nervousness.

"Are you…comfortable with everything we're doing?"

"Very," she replies immediately, a cheeky grin crossing her face as her head bobs up and down in affirmation.

"Have you perhaps…been single for a while?"

The nodding stops and a look of trepidation crosses her face, her eyes not quite meeting mine, her hand sliding off my cock.

"Am I doing something wrong?"

Fuck. Some asshole has crushed her confidence, or worse.

"No, of course not," I'm quick to rush out at the same time she quietly blurts, "I haven't done this before."

Wait. What?

"Repeat that."

She doesn't, but her shoulder hitches in a tiny insolent shrug, her chin set at a defiant angle.

It can't be. *She* can't be. She's a bit unsure sexually, yes. A tad. But I thought it was due to my being her boss or the difference in our ages. An adult relationship versus a college one. How can this grown woman, a woman who sucked me off in my office, still be a virgin? Yet, it helps explain her deviations between sultry temptress and innocent farm girl. The enthusiasm mixed with nerves. The anxiety about the size of my dick.

"You're a virgin?" I say, because apparently I need to hear myself say it out loud in order to wrap my mind around it.

Some guys fantasize about this shit, I know. But right now, all I feel is a weight. A weight, and confusion. This girl shouldn't be here, losing her virginity to me of all people. She should have lost it in some barn to her high school sweetheart.

Speaking of which.

I've been jealous of her high school boyfriend for no reason, as it turns out.

But I should be walking away. I did what I came for. I took her to dinner. I gave her the mind-blowing orgasm I owed her. And now, I could walk her out, hand her off to Leo, and have him drive her home. Then I could hit the shower and jack the fuck off until I come, and that could be the end of it.

But then I look at her, and…there's no chance of that happening.

She's perfect, watching me with her shining brown eyes, her bottom lip tucked into her mouth as she watches me process this. A little furrow across her forehead. Her hair's falling out of the loose bun she'd pulled it into earlier and she's crossed her arms across her chest, a defensive, protective gesture because she's taking my reaction as judgement or rejection.

And then there's the way, even now, that she's looking at me. She wants me. She wants to be here. I want her here.

Fuck the rest of it.

"Emery," I say , brushing a wisp of hair off her forehead as my eyes dart to the condom on the nightstand. "Do you want to do this?"

"More than anything," she whispers, and some of the tension in her shoulders relaxes. "I wanted you the very first day I spilled coffee all over you. I couldn't stop imagining doing this with you."

Well then. I'm not made of stone for fuck's sake.

We come together in a frenzy of kisses, hungry and burning with our twin desires. Her hands slide down my body until she reaches my cock, and then she grips me firmly as her tongue slides over mine.

"Please," she begs. "Please, please."

I don't need to be asked again. I grab the condom and slide it on while she watches. The look on her face, eager. But her ankles betray her nerves because they've crossed themselves again, causing me to fight back a grin. God, I could take her so many ways. But what would feel the best for her? I've never thought about that before. My high school girlfriend was a virgin, but so was I at the time so that's hardly a reference point. Besides that experience was…a while ago. I've had no shortage of practice since, but with experienced women. And now, as my balls throb with the need to erupt, I know I'll need to take it slow. I'll have to ease her into it.

I have to make this good for her.

Both from a point of vanity and practicality. If I don't make it good then she could have just done this with anyone.

"Relax," I tell her, with a pointed look at her legs. She rolls her eyes, exhaling a small laugh at herself as she complies. Her lashes flutter against her cheeks as I slide between her legs and kiss her breasts, sucking on those perfect, hard nipples as she shivers beneath me. I kiss my way down, and down again until I'm between her thighs again. I lick her still sensitive clit once and feel her squirm with delight. Her body's ready and aching for more, and I'm past ready to give it to her.

Still, slow is the name of the game. I slide one finger into her, and she clenches around the single digit, but she's slick and eager to take more. I give her a second finger to gently stretch her, and she moans, bucking against me.

"Now," she demands. "Now."

I smirk. "Still so impatient."

Her eyes fly open. "I can't take it anymore, Harrison. I need you inside me. Now."

"Hush. I'm the boss here," I widen my fingers inside her, stretching her further, working her clit with my thumb.

"Literally," she quips, squirming beneath me.

I toy with her for another minute as payback for her impertinence. But only for a minute, because my own restraint is waning.

I move on top of her, pressing my forehead to hers for a brief moment before we proceed. Our eyes lock and then she slides a hand behind my neck and pulls my lips to hers.

I'm not sure who's reassuring who.

I palm my length and ease forward, pressing at her entrance. This is it. There's no going back. She shimmies her hips closer to me, pressing against my cock. I drive forward, so slowly I worry I'm going to cause myself permanent damage. Jesus, I want to sink into her, balls deep. Fast. Repeatedly. And right fucking now.

"Relax," I remind her, pressing forward another inch. She wiggles, which apparently helps her relax but I can assure you, does nothing to help me. "How is that," I hiss between clenched teeth.

"Good. More." Another wiggle, God help me.

She's so fucking wet and slick, but tight.

I slip a hand under her thigh and spread her wider, one knee bent toward her chest. Her lips form a silent "oh," as I shove forward another inch.

"Still good?"

She nods, but her face is tense.

"You're just so big," she comments, and her tone implies it's a bit of a complaint.

"You won't always be complaining about that." I grin, pressing a quick kiss to her forehead, bracing myself above her.

"If you say so." She wrinkles her nose and wiggles beneath me yet again. But this time, the moment she adjusts and relaxes I surge forward, sinking in to the hilt.

Her mouth falls open and she emits a very verbal "oh!" this time. Her eyes squeeze shut and her fingers dig into my forearms as her body adjusts to accommodate me.

We fit together perfectly, whatever she may think of my size. But I hold myself still over her, waiting for her to signal she's good. I'm rewarded a moment later.

"More," she says, opening her eyes and unclenching her fingertips from my arms. She adds a little nod and her hands slide up my arms to my shoulders. Her expression is a heady mix of surprise and lust.

She sighs, little moans of pleasure emitting from her throat when I pull halfway out and slide in again. I'm careful to watch her reactions with each thrust, each adjustment I make to the angle. But being inside her is a drug of its own, and it's hard to focus and keep from pounding into her too hard. I want more. So much more.

She must be thinking the same thing, because she bucks up against me and wraps both of her legs over my hips, pulling me down so that I'm deeper still. She cries out as my cock drives inside her, but then we move together, two bodies put into motion, and it's perfect and I can't hold back any longer.

I speed up the pace, but Emery is right there with me. My orgasm shakes my entire body, rolling over me with force, sending me to the stars and back down to earth as I empty myself inside of her. It isn't just sex, not just a release, but a separation from who I was before and the person I am, now, with her in this moment. It feels impossible, but then I feel her come again, too, against me, and I lose myself completely in the moment. We rock together as we both finish, and then, I collapse on top of her before rolling us over so I don't crush her. We're both breathing heavily from the exertion.

For a moment, neither of us speak. We just breathe. I run my hand along her side, and then cup her jaw as I pull her in for a kiss. She smiles against my lips and then leans back so that I can see her wide eyes, her face heady with spent lust.

"Oh my God," she says. "Does...does it feel like that every time?"

I laugh. "It can if you're with me."

"Was I supposed to come that much?" She shakes her head, and manages to eye me with a lot of suspicion for a virgin who just came three times. "It felt like more than my fair share," she adds.

"You're fine. There's a sliding scale for orgasms," I tell her. "In the name of equality."

"A measuring system where I get more but we're even?" She quirks a brow, a smile tugging at her lips. "I guess that's okay."

I wind a strand of her hair between my fingers as she drops her head to my chest.

"Oh my God," she repeats. "I cannot wait to do that again."

The words are warm, settling against me in the afterglow of sex. I feel her chest rise and fall, knowing that I did that. I brought her that pleasure. Perhaps her virginity was wasted on me, but I made it good for her. Which makes us even. Sort of. Maybe? I can please her again. And again, all night, as much as she wants.

Because tonight, nothing stands between us.

She's mine.

CHAPTER EIGHTEEN

WHEN I WAKE UP, both revitalized and groggy from last night's events, I instinctively reach over for Emery's body. I got so used to it last night, finding its curves and dips, that I feel like I know it better than my own. It feels like she should be here, always, in my bed, but her side is empty, the covers thrown back and the sheets rumpled.

Did she leave in the middle of the night? Sneak out and call a Lyft to that tiny apartment of hers? Was she ashamed when she woke up next to me, her boss? Did she realize she made a mistake?

But then I hear faint sounds of life from the kitchen. The smell of coffee wafts into the room, and I realize that this girl is making herself at home in my home. I don't dare to think that she's feeling the way I do, like she belongs here. Besides, those are ridiculous thoughts, the leftover product of a night's hard fucking. Sentimental bullshit that I thought I'd successfully excised from my life before, creeping back in even though I know better.

She was hungry and caffeine-deprived. She's a smart enough girl to know how the kitchen works. That's all there is to it.

I check the clock. It's early, but not as early as I like to get up. Normally, I'd hop on the treadmill in my home gym for a quick run to burn off steam before work, but there's no time for that. I hop in the shower, letting the water and steam wake me up completely. You'd think that, after last night, my cock would be plenty satisfied, but the thought of her, still here, still in my home, sends blood pumping straight to it leaving me with throbbing morning wood.

This is a problem. She's a problem. Last night's fucking should've driven the need for her completely out of my mind. She's just an intern, a cute, hot-as-fuck intern that any human with a dick would crave. And now, that's done, and she should be out of my system.

Except she's not. And more than that, the more I replay last night and think about how she felt, smelled, and tasted, the more I realize that that girl is just as addicting as that coffee she likes to spill on me.

"You know, I can take care of that."

I turn and see her standing there in my robe, the one I like to leave on the chair in my bedroom in case I need to get up and pace in the middle of the night. I don't always sleep well, and often, an idea will force me out of bed, and I'll spend hours lapping the house to sort it out. I've never seen the robe on another person. It's so big on her that it reaches the floor, even though it's short on me. It's unbelted, hanging open revealing a slice of her naked form beneath. I can't help but think she unbelted it on purpose, the little tease.

Her eyes are staring at my rock-hard cock, and her tongue slides across her lips as she examines me. Apparently, she's not feeling sated either. She's pink with lust, from her lips to her kiss-bruised lips. She slowly shrugs the robe off her shoulders, watching me as she does. Gauging my reaction, as if I might stop her. As if I might pass on shower sex. God she's new. As if any man would turn down assistance with a hard-on in the shower. Finally, she lets it drop to the floor, standing naked before me. One knee slightly bent, the toes of her foot flexing on the tile.

Every remaining pint of blood in me rushes to my cock, hardening me to the point of bursting. She opens the shower door and steps inside, and immediately, we crush together, our mouths hungrily devouring one another, like two people starving on a desert island where the only sustenance is each other.

"Oh," she whispers into my ear as she grabs my cock in her hand. It looks so huge in her hand as she pumps the slick, wet flesh.

"I thought you might be tired from last night," I say.

"Me? Or this perfect cock?" Emery says, pausing to fondle my balls, so full and sensitive that the lightest touch makes me groan.

"I'm not tired," she says when I can't form words. "I want to be fucked."

I flip her so that she's standing pressed against the glass, fitting myself behind her so that my cock is jutting against her back. I bite and nibble at her neck and earlobes as she purrs with delight, and then I move my hand to her pussy, siding a finger between her plump lips, then plunging inside. She's wet and waiting for me, and she clenches around me as her thighs buckle. I fuck her with my hand as I grind my cock against her back, kissing her neck and making her moan.

"Fuck me," she begs. "Fuck me now."

"I can't fuck you now, you impatient minx," I say. "Not without protection."

She growls in frustration, bucking her hips against my finger. With my thumb, I rub small, frantic circles against the tight bud of nerves of her clit, and she cries out at the sensation. I add a second finger, pumping it in and out of her as I work my thumb. She's putty in my hands, and her orgasm shakes her entire body as I press her forward, her body vibrating with my hard cock trapped between us against her back.

I turn the shower off, and carry her still wet, shaking body to the bathroom counter. She whines and paws at me, and I know she's dying for my cock, just as much as I'm dying to give it to her. I fling open a cabinet drawer and grab one of the black and gold packets stored inside, ripping it open and sliding it over my dick. I'm grateful for the thin rubber sheath that'll help me to not come immediately inside her, since that's what my dick's currently begging to do.

"Now," she pants. "Fuck, Harrison, I can't wait. Now."

I lift her legs around me so that she can pull me close, but I don't enter her, not yet. I let my dick rub against the still tender, swollen clit, teasing the lips of her pussy as I rain kisses down on her neck and her breasts. I lick at her nipples and swirl my tongue around them as she groans. She buries her hands in my damp hair and pulls my mouth to her own, as our tongues collide with lust.

"Harrison," she begs. "Harrison, please."

That's when I push inside of her. I push so deep that she cries again, and then I remember that she's still new at this, and likely sore from last night. I thrust slowly until I feel her pussy grow slicker and slicker, letting her take each generous inch of my dick until I'm all the way inside of her, pounding against her as she leans back on the counter and arches her back. She keeps pushing her hips higher, angling for that perfect pairing between us, and I grab the cheeks of her supple ass and hoist her up so that we're joined in exactly the right places. As our thighs slap together, she moans out my name again and again, and I know I was right last night about her. She's an addiction, and I'm completely at her mercy.

How could I not be? She's perfect now, so lost in the moment, her facial features twisting, tits bouncing as I slam into her again and again. Her pussy welcomes my cock deeper than I thought possible, clenching and tightening around me. Her hand finds her clit as she follows the moves I used last night, stroking up and down in time with my thrusts.

She comes around me, shaking and convulsing and wild with lust. Her climax pushes me over the edge and into my own, and with a single, "Fuck!" I let my own orgasm go, releasing into her, the feeling rolling over me like a tidal wave. For a moment after, we just sit there, clinging to one another, me still inside of her, each of us breathing as if we've just been given new life.

I look into those wide brown eyes and find the kind of deep connection that I'd written off as no longer possible. I see a person who looks and sees me and still wants more. We can get back in the shower and wash off the evidence of what just happened, but the mark of it, the connection between us, that isn't going to disappear down the drain.

Because, I realize with a jolt, I have marked her. I'd been a fool to think this could be a one-time thing, an exchange of orgasms to clear my ledger of responsibility. I'll never be just a name on a list of suitors for her. I'll always be her first, bold-faced and underlined in her personal history.

I've stamped her in a way no man ever has, or ever will, again.

The thought leaves me raw and, ridiculously, happy. As if this is a place I want to exist, forever, for her.

She's dangerous. And this is unmarked ground. So why am I so ready to slide off the cliff?

CHAPTER NINETEEN

AFTER WE FINISH, I leave her to shower on her own. It takes a lot of resisting on both of our parts for me to walk away from her naked body, but I know if we don't get moving we'll never make it to work on time. I could call Sandy and give her an excuse, but I know that if we both show up late, people will talk and put it together.

Especially Ramon. I can already imagine the conversation he'd want to have with me after putting together the pieces. I'd bet he'd go on again about my company and what I've built and the unnecessary threats to that. He'd point out that this isn't part of the plan.

Of course, Emery isn't part of the plan, and that's exactly the problem. But there's no use thinking about that now. I just need to get us out of the house.

When I get out to the kitchen I see that I was right about Emery making herself right at home. She's made herself breakfast, pans I never use are on the stove, the remnants of egg and vegetables left behind. She must have used the ingredients that Hector, my chef, had stocked in my fridge. I'll have to let him know that I've actually used the groceries and that he'll need to restock if he planned to use these later.

Normally, he comes right before I get off of work and has the meals ready for me as soon as I get home. Then, of course, he leaves, and I eat by myself, generally while poring over my laptop as I try to get ahead of the next day.

Hector never makes breakfast, though. Breakfast is always a hard-boiled egg and black coffee to go. I look and see that Emery's also made coffee, and I pour myself a cup as I continue to investigate the utter mess that the girl has left in my kitchen.

This isn't the neat and tidy cooking that Hector does. Actually, I guess I don't know what the kitchen looks like while Hector cooks. He always cleans up before I get home. But I can't imagine neat and precise Hector cooking this way, with three different pots and pans out, egg shells on the counter, random utensils scattered around. It's the sort of mess I would normally despise, and yet…for some reason, I'm not even annoyed. I'm probably too surprised to be annoyed. That's it.

"Oh, sorry," Emery's voice calls out. I turn and see that she's in a towel, padding toward me, hair still damp.

"I got a little carried away," she says. "But don't worry. I made you one, too."

"You made me what?"

"A breakfast burrito. I hope you like eggs. I used the stuff that was in your fridge." She pauses to take a breath and grin, but then keeps on talking. "I put it in the warming drawer for you. Did you know you have a warming drawer? I've never seen one outside of one of those kitchen renovation shows and I used to think the idea sounded kind of ridiculous, because hello microwave, but it's kind of nice actually."

Never, not once, did Blythe cook for me. Ever. It was something beneath both of us, something other people did. And besides, could we have made anything better than the best chefs in New York? Of course not. So we didn't bother.

In fact, the last time someone cooked for me, it must have

been my dad. Pizza nights. It's been so long since we had them that I can barely remember them. But at one time, when I was a boy, we made pizza together. The memory's sharp and sudden of us in the kitchen, him showing me how to knead the dough to the edges. He taught me to use crushed tomatoes, nothing canned.

The memory pulls me up short, and I turn away from Emery so that she can't see the expression on my face.

"Shoot," she says. "Sorry. I guess I made a mess. And I didn't ask about using your cookware. They looked sort of expensive—"

I laugh. Sort of expensive. I'm sure every pan in my kitchen is top of the line, but she wouldn't care. Again and again, the girl shows her true colors. I think of her tiny apartment. There's probably a set of communal pans, hand-me-downs or gifts that are burnt on the edges.

"What?" Emery asks, touching my arm to turn me around. "Did I overstep? Should I not—I'm sorry, Harrison."

My name again. God, she's going to be the end of me.

"No," I say, trying to recover from this ridiculous moment. It was so much easier in the shower, fucking her senseless. With sex, the rules are simple. Give and take. She has an orgasm, I have one. But here, in my kitchen, she's made me breakfast, and now, she's standing here in my towel. I don't have a playbook for this situation. And then there's the fact that I have to figure out a way to get us both to work without replaying every HR scandal in the book.

"No, you didn't," I say, turning back to her. "We're just running late."

"Right," she says. "Well, good thing I made a burrito. You can eat it on the way to work."

I smirk. "You think I'm going to eat a breakfast burrito on the way to work? In my suit?"

She shrugs. "No? Why not? You have a driver so your hands are free."

Of course. The girl who plopped her ass down on a cement planter to eat food from a cart wouldn't see a problem with eating a breakfast burrito in a Burberry suit.

"I know you've taken a liking to spilling coffee on me," I say. "But I do generally try to avoid changing clothes at work."

"About that," she says. "Or sort of about that. I'm going to be late for work because I don't think yesterday's date outfit is appropriate for the office."

Shit. She's right.

The unfortunate thing is that I do have women's clothes here. Blythe emptied out her closet—or, more accurately, paid someone else to empty out her closet—but she left a decent amount of clothing. Probably as a "fuck you" to me, another chore for me to have to deal with on her behalf. But right now, it might just come in handy.

"I have some things here," I say. "My ex-wife left some stuff behind, if you want to borrow something to wear."

Emery bites her lip. "Won't she notice if I show up wearing her clothes? And isn't that…weird?"

I shrug. "It's mostly a bunch of stuff she's never even worn. Things her personal shopper sent with the tags still on."

Emery thinks about this. "I guess that would be okay. Besides, we could've shopped at the same store, right?"

She says it with a smile, and I hold back a laugh. Somehow, I don't think Emery's been shopping at the same places as Blythe. Not unless Target and Chanel have somehow merged into the same store.

I walk her back upstairs to the room that I've had all of Blythe's former possessions shoved into. Suits and dresses and tops and even brand new lingerie, most of which was sent by designers. They're all hung on silver hangers in a closet that stretches back, complete with poufs and mirrors that glitter in the perfect lighting. In the drawers, there are also unopened makeup tubes and palettes that I tell Emery to help herself to, and her eyes widen at the selection.

"You mean I can just...take these?"

"Why not? No one else is going to use them."

"But won't she..." Emery pauses, carefully assembling the words together. "Won't she miss these? Doesn't she want them?"

"Emery," I say. "I promise you, she's already taken everything she wants. She probably doesn't even know what's here. Or she assumes I burned whatever was left." I should have. Like a spiritual cleansing.

She runs her hand through a long silky dress before glancing back at me. She's still in that damn towel, and the fabric dips slightly as she moves her arm. A growl forms in my throat and my cock twitches, but I force myself to ignore both signs of want. Thankfully, it's actually relatively easy to do here in the graveyard of things that once belonged to my ex.

"You really hate each other, don't you?" Emery says.

I sigh. I don't want to get into it, talking about Blythe this early in the morning. But with her doe eyes watching me, waiting for a response, I don't really have a choice.

"She hated that I kept the apartment," I admit. "She tried to tell me she deserved to keep it. As if I was the one that ruined our marriage. As if she pays a cent on this place."

"Where did she go?" Emery asks. "I mean, not that I feel bad for her or anything. I just meant, did she find anywhere to stay?"

I snort. "Do you really think I just kicked her to the curb? She's in another apartment I own a few blocks away. It was supposed to be an investment property, but here we are. It was important to me to keep this apartment. I can't quite explain it."

I could explain it, actually, but I don't want to. Maybe it makes me an asshole, but she took so much already. I wanted to take something from her. But none of that makes me sound like a decent guy. And besides, Blythe will own that apartment free and clear as soon as I sign the divorce papers. She's making out just fine.

"It's stupid big," Emery notes. Clearly she had a peek around the place on her way to make breakfast.

"It is," I agree, because what else can I say. It is stupid big. It was bigger than we needed for two people, let alone one. It was meant for a couple with a future.

"Do you think…" Emery starts, then bites her lip, pulling back whatever question she was going to ask.

"What?" I ask, sounding more defensive than I mean to. Whenever it comes to Blythe, there's always a part of me that's waiting to be accused of being a jerk. Maybe that's because Blythe tried—and continues to try—so damn hard to convince me that I am one.

"Nothing," Emery says. "It's too personal."

I should leave it there. If we're going to recover from last night and move on, we need to keep our personal lives out of it. Leave the feelings out of it, the probing questions. I already know too much about her, and she knows even more about me. And yet, I can't stop myself.

"What?" I ask. "What were you going to say?"

"I just…I was going to ask if you think you would have stayed together," she says. "If she didn't cheat."

Her question sinks into the air between us, waiting there like a landmine for me to activate. For a moment, all I can think about is Blythe's endless parade of accusations after I found her and Robert together. The ones about how it was my fault.

Now we really are too personal. These are feelings I don't even want to touch, let alone discuss with Emery.

"I don't know," I deflect. And then, before she can say anything else, I add, "But it doesn't matter. We don't live in the world of 'what if.' The reality is that I've got some clothes for you to pick out. So take whatever you want."

I leave her in the closet to go and pace in my living room. Her question has disturbed me. It's not like it isn't one that I haven't asked myself. Were the signs there all along between Blythe and me? She certainly would like to think so, that it's my fault for being too invested in the job. Too separate. Not attentive enough to her, to the marriage.

But those are all lies. In fact, if I wanted to answer Emery's question honestly, I think that, maybe, I could have gotten past the cheating. It happens sometimes in a marriage, doesn't it? Not all marriages. But people make mistakes. Someone gets too drunk, maybe. A slipup. It's not something that I think I could have easily stomached, but if Blythe was honest and came to me, maybe we could have moved past it. Maybe? But she didn't.

First, she lied and said what I walked in on was a one-time thing. Then she said it was a week. Then a month. Then a few months. Pulling the truth out of her was like using pliers on a rotten tooth, and even once I'd managed to get it out of her, she covered the lies with more emotional manipulation. I'd seen her persuade and sweet talk our clients into deals, but I'd never imagined she'd try to turn those powers on me.

"Harrison, you're the one who wanted the divorce," she told me once. "You pushed me away."

"Right into the bed of my best friend?" I'd shot back, and that had silenced her. Temporarily, at least.

But that's it, isn't it? The real reason that Blythe and I aren't together anymore is because she lied, not just about the affair, but everything. What she wanted from me, what she wanted from the company. And she's going to keep lying, even now with the charity, until everything around her is rubble. The idea fills me with such rage that I'm tempted to walk into that closet and actually burn everything in there like I joked about. But I won't. Emery's here, and I told her the truth. Those clothes mean nothing to Blythe. I'd be setting off the smoke alarms for nothing.

Still, the longer Emery's here, and the more her comments about Blythe fester inside of me, the more the reality of what transpired last night settles on me. I'd thought this would be an easy exchange, repaying the orgasm she gave me with one —or more—of her own. But now, my kitchen is full of pans she used to make breakfast. To make me breakfast.

How will we be able to maintain professionalism at the office? Is she going to be clingy? Expectant? Blushing at me whenever I walk down the halls? Before last night, she was throwing herself at me, but now that we've actually sealed the deal—and now that I've taken her fucking virginity— what happens next? And these complicated feelings of mine will need to be tamped down, too.

Even if I'm not sure I want them to be.

How I handle the next few hours is key. I'll need to make sure she knows that this doesn't change anything at work. That I'm still her boss. That she'll need to respect boundaries. After all, isn't that why I took her out in the first place? To get the fucking out of our systems so that we could go back to living our separate lives?

It was.

It is.

It just took a few more rounds than I expected, I decide. That's all.

So then, what do I do next? Do we arrive at work in the same car? No, that's impossible. Any suit off the street would be able to tell that we'd spent the night together. We'll have to arrive separately. Do I call another car? Do I drop her off a few blocks from the building like her damn dad that she's ashamed to be seen with?

The answer's obvious. I need to let her fend for herself. Leave her downstairs to call an Uber or a Lyft or a taxi or whatever people use these days. The goddamned subway won't kill her. Then she can arrive late and blame it on, I don't know, her phone dying or something.

So why don't I just tell her that? Why do I care about how cold and indifferent that sounds?

"I'm ready!"

I pause from my pacing and turn to see her, standing before me in a light gray pencil skirt that skims her ass and a flowy purple blouse. She's pulled her hair up and is wearing bright red lipstick, so different on her than whatever she usually wears. She looks...powerful. Is it the clothes? Or is it something about being here with me? It's probably her newfound sexual confidence. She's very nearly glowing, and I'm not sure how I feel about that. She'll be a magnet to anyone with a dick.

"Is it too much?" Emery asks, touching a finger to the lipstick. "I've never tried it before. I thought it might be fun?"

I don't have anything to say to that. What can I say? That I love how she looks? That I want to call in sick to my own company so I can spend the entire day exploring all the ways I can make her orgasm?

Fuck.

"I'll blot it off," she says, and before I can stop her, she's grabbed a tissue from her purse and swiped most of it. She reapplies some lip balm on top, and even though her lips still look slightly red, almost bruised, it's not as severe as before. She looks more like herself.

"We need to go," I say, still struggling with what to say to her.

"Lead the way," she chirps. "And don't forget your burrito."

Right. The food she made for me. My stomach churns at the thought, and I tell myself it's because I'm still worried about setting boundaries.

"I'll reheat it later," I say. "I'm not really a breakfast person."

"But—"

"Ms. Mills, we really are running late," I say.

I don't mean it to sound cold, but I can tell by the way that her face falls that she takes it that way. Without another word, she nods and walks ahead of me to the door. I follow, grabbing my briefcase as I go.

We're quiet in the elevator as it zooms down. I'll need to fix this. But she must understand that this wasn't a personal slight. We are two people who had a sexual encounter, and now it's time to move along. I don't need her breakfast. I don't need her to take care of me. That isn't what this is.

Leo's waiting at the curb per usual, and thankfully, the old man doesn't comment when Emery slides into the car with me. She sits on the far left and I sit on the far right, and she is smiling and friendly with Leo, asking about his morning and his plans for the rest of the day. I force myself to tune out their conversation and instead scroll through my phone. My work emails are safe, full of problems that are easy to solve and don't involve Emery or her doe eyes. Of course, there's also Claire's ever-present request to go over options for the divorce papers, but I ignore that, too.

"We're here, sir," Leo calls, unnecessarily, as we arrive at the building.

I hesitate. Now is the moment. How do I tell Emery that we'll need to be discreet? How do I introduce this dance?

"Ms. Mills—"

"Mr. Duke," she smoothly cuts in, and it stings. The Mr. Duke shit.

"I need to make a call," I mutter.

She makes a disgusted sound from her throat and climbs over me, because I realize too late that I'm on the goddamned curb side of the car, in New York City traffic, and I'm just sitting there like an idiot while I insinuate she should get out of the car without me.

Leo's look in the rearview mirror does nothing to help my mood.

"Have a wonderful day, Mr. Duke," she says, not even looking at me as she steps out of the car and slams the door shut behind her. She clicks her way to the building, without a single look back.

Well.

So what do I do now? Trail after her like a scolded dog? I do not trail after anyone, least of all an intern. Even if that intern is *her*.

"Leo, could you do a lap?" I ask. "I need to make a few calls."

Leo doesn't argue. He doesn't even shoot me another of his meaningful looks in the rearview mirror. He just pulls away from the curb, nodding as he says, "Yes, sir."

I scroll through my phone and dial one of the clients who emailed this morning. Business. That's what I need to crush this from my mind.

Even if, during the entire call, Emery still looms front and center.

CHAPTER TWENTY

MY OFFICE IS cold when I walk into it. Something must be wrong with the air conditioner because it's practically an ice box when I walk inside. I leave my suit jacket on and take a seat at my computer, massaging at my temples as I try to transition firmly into Duke Capital and its safe world of numbers and distractions. Unfortunately, once my computer revives, there are remnants of last night in the form of restaurant menus still lingering in my open internet tabs. I close them all quickly. There are also a number of sticky notes on my desk with scribbled names of charities that I was looking into, but those aren't so easy to get rid of because I still haven't figured out what to do there.

I tell myself I'm overthinking. It doesn't matter how it ended this morning. In fact, it might be better that it was messy. Now we can move along as planned. After all, Emery certainly was quick to put up her own walls in the car. The cynical businessman in me wonders if she realized that I wasn't immediately going to start fawning over her and offer her a promotion because we fucked. Though if she had, it would have been very out of character with the innocent farm girl that I know. In fact, I've never met a person who seems so in love with the simple things before. Her simple apartment, food from a street vendor, homemade breakfast, mind-blowing orgasms.

Fine, the orgasms weren't simple. I need to focus. On business. Because I'm already far too distracted with Emery. I have to separate the business from the pleasure, and it should be easy once I get started on the day. The calls I made from my car helped me get the ball rolling on some new possibilities, so I decide to start there.

I text Ramon to tell him to stop by when he has a moment, which we both know means I'd like to talk now. Thankfully, I must catch him when he isn't busy, because he pops up shortly in my office. There are a few bags under his eyes, and he's clutching the largest coffee possible like it's his lifeblood. The consequence of having young kids, I'd guess. But he still has an easy smile as he takes a seat across from me.

"Hey there, boss," he says. "You beckoned?"

I did. I need to ask Ramon about the new opportunity he was looking into for me. I should also get his thoughts on some of the marketing that we've been putting together for Pink. But once he walked in, my gaze landed on the sticky notes on my desk, the ones with the charities.

He asked me before what he could do to help. And maybe, just maybe, getting this charity issue solved will put Emery out of my mind for good.

"I need your advice on a sensitive matter," I say. "Related to the charity arm of Duke Capital. And I'll need your utmost discretion."

Ramon blinks. "The charity department? Aren't we usually…hands off in that area?"

He's tiptoeing around it. He knows what everybody else does. That I avoid Blythe and her department like the plague. But even if Blythe wasn't willing to play ball with me the other day, I can't let it go. I need to find a way to make this right.

"You asked what Blythe and I were arguing about the other day," I say. "To be honest, I've got some concerns. Real concerns, about which charities we're backing."

I fill him in about everything I know, from the rating to the massive overhead and the pittance of money that actually makes its way to kids. Ramon's face changes as I talk. The tired expression falls away, leaving indignation and then anger as he realizes what I'm saying.

"Well, what did Bly—what did Ms. Lawrence-Duke say about this?"

I laugh. "What do you think she said? And apparently, Robert had plenty to do with it, too. He's got family on the board. But if we pull out now, we look like we're taking funds from kids. And Blythe says any scandal I try to bring down on her will end up on me and the rest of the company."

Ramon considers this. "There's got to be another solution. Another way we can drive money to the right charity. Did you have any ideas?"

"A few possibilities but nothing concrete," I say. "I think it's important that we look for charities that might normally fly under the radar. The bigger, flashier ones are already getting the funds they need. We need to really look for the ones that need the support."

Ramon nods. "Completely agree. I can look into it."

He pulls out his phone and jots some notes down. Then, he hesitates and looks back at me.

"There is something else I think you should know, boss," he says. "And I'm afraid it's not great news."

Immediately, it's like ice coursing through my veins. Someone must have seen Emery get out of my car this morning. God, maybe even Blythe. Was she entering the building at exactly the right time? Or did she see Emery in the halls and somehow put it together that she and I spent the night with one another? *That's ridiculous*, I chastise myself. Did she actually recognize the blouse Emery is wearing as something she might have ordered forever ago and forgotten about? Also ridiculous.

Part of me thrills at that last part though. It's a petty part, one that wants her to know that she means nothing to me, that I'll recycle her possessions however I see fit. But—I also meant what I said when I gave them to Emery. Blythe doesn't even know what's still at our apartment. My apartment. She likely didn't even select any of that stuff, having shoppers who did that for her. Having so much that leaving half of it, brand new with tags, was irrelevant.

They're just clothes, and someone should get to wear them. Especially someone like Emery. Though…yeah, it's weird. I should arrange to have the rest of it donated.

I swallow and wait for Ramon to drop the HR bomb on me. He sighs.

"There's a chance that Monica's pulling on the Pink deal with us," he says. "Apparently, someone else is pursuing them and might be offering a better deal."

"What?" I say, because this truly was the last thing I was expecting. "I thought that was nearly wrapped up?"

"There's a small chance of it going south," Ramon says. "Thus far, it's just a rumor I heard. And it could be nothing. But apparently, there's another company who is trying to pitch them. I think they're suggesting that they understand women better than, well, we do."

I bark out a laugh. "That's impossible. At every single one of our meetings, Monica's loved our ideas. I should just get her on the phone right now and sort this out."

"I think we need to be more subtle about this," Ramon says. "Like I said, this could be nothing. But I know they're going to be at the Sun Valley Conference next week, and you know whoever is trying to poach them will be there too. It would be good for us to have eyes on the ground there. Your eyes, frankly."

I was already planning to go. The Sun Valley Conference

has always been one of the places to be seen for anyone serious about business. It's known as the "billionaires conference" for good reason, and as the billionaire in question at Duke Capital, I would never miss it.

"Beyond that," Ramon says. "It might be good to bring someone on the team who could...well, lend a female perspective. Make it clear that we value the voices of women at Duke Capital."

"Blythe will already be there," I say, trying not to sound too bitter. Blythe always goes to represent our philanthropic group, though this year, I wish she wouldn't. There's no telling what she'll be sinking us into.

"Maybe someone else," Ramon suggests.

I stare at him, not following.

"One of the reasons Monica was so keen on us in the first place was because you asked Emery for her opinion in that meeting," Ramon says. "What if you take her along?"

I bristle. "I'm not bringing an intern just to make it look like we have women at the company. We have plenty of female executives."

"But she's the one Monica will recognize and remember," Ramon says. "I guarantee it. And you liked what she said, didn't you? And you said she was a big help at the charity event. Clearly, you respect her. So why not?"

I sigh. "You know why not, Ramon."

"Harrison," Ramon says, his voice growing serious. "I'm going to assume you told me the truth and that whatever went on in the break room was a one-time, weak moment and that you know better. Your company's on the line. She's a smart girl, but you've made it clear to me she's not someone you plan on having a future with. So what could be the problem?"

I think about it. Everything Ramon's saying makes perfect sense, but it still feels jumbled in my mind. Something about it feels wrong. Probably because the one-time thing is a lie.

Due to having slept with her last night. Twice. And again this morning.

"I'll go alone," I say. "I'll figure out another way. But I appreciate you getting the scoop on this info about Pink, Ramon."

Ramon nods. "I understand. You know best."

He stands to leave. I tap at my computer, now with fresh problems to solve. I'd always planned on going to the conference, but it feels more important now. Usually, my preparation doesn't need to be as complicated. But now, I'll need to focus on Pink for the rest of the week.

"I'll look into the charity issue, too," he says. "We'll fix it, Harrison."

I nod. I appreciate it that he's as upset as I am. If anything, it reassures me that I'm doing this because I'm invested in the company. Because I care about the right things.

I spend the rest of the morning and afternoon deep in research mode, holed up in my office cave. But eventually, I leave to get some fresh air and check in with some of the executives around the office. I always want my employees to see me as someone who is visible and involved, not just the guy who delegates decisions. I might not be the warmest CEO, but I'm knowledgeable, and that's key to earning respect.

On my way back to my desk, I see her. It was inevitable, of course. And, fuck it, maybe I wanted to see her. I blame the irresponsible side of me for the urge, the one led by my dick rather than my mind. But there she is, talking with Sandy at Sandy's desk, leaning forward so that the full curve of her ass is on display in that perfect gray skirt. Immediately, the memories of this morning and last night resurface, and I remember the feel of my own body pressed against hers and how perfectly goddamned soft her skin is. The way I pounded into her. The perfect bounce of her tits. The sounds she made.

My cock twitches and I start to look away, but her eyes

find mine. There's hurt there that I caused with my asshole behavior. And Ramon's words are echoing in my mind, how he believes I know better than to get involved with her. That I'm a mature professional, a man who could have anyone he wants. Anyone appropriate.

So why am I fixated on wanting her?

"Ms. Mills," I say, pausing at Sandy's desk. "I was hoping I could have a word with you. I'd like to discuss a conference opportunity with you."

It's stupid, so stupid, but it's the first thing that comes to my mind. Besides, saying it in front of Sandy gives me an excuse to get her into my office so that I can apologize for earlier. It also shows Sandy that I have a purely professional interest in Emery and lays the groundwork for any future rumors. If anyone asks, I'm mentoring. That's all.

One look at Sandy and her smirk tells me she thinks that's all bullshit, but I decide to ignore it.

Emery stares at me, not speaking. The phone in her hand buzzes and she glances at it, her eyes widening before she flips the screen over. I wonder if it's more student loan problems. Or maybe she's been texting one of her roommates about her dick of a boss and the night she had. But no. I don't think so. Emery's never struck me as a gossip.

"Of course," she says, clutching the phone in one hand, a coffee in the other. "After you, Mr. Duke."

We shut the door behind us, but I give her a wide berth as I walk to my desk. She's not the seductive minx from before, prowling into my space. She stands close to the door, still looking concerned.

"Are you going to spill that on me?" I ask, nodding towards her coffee with a smirk. Great icebreaker.

She glances at the paper cup in her hand, as if she'd forgotten about it, then shrugs, a tiny hitch of her shoulder. "No. I need this one. I didn't get much sleep last night," she adds, her tone dry.

"I wanted to apologize," I tell her. "I wasn't myself this morning. I think I may have been...unkind to you."

She blinks, clearly not having anticipated this. "Oh."

"Your questions about my ex-wife, well, they unsettled me," I admit. "She's not someone I like to think about, and yet, with you, I find that I keep talking about her."

"I'm sorry that I keep bringing her up," she says. "I didn't mean—"

"No," I say, again, too harsh. "I didn't mean that. I just meant that I'm not used to talking about her. The separation. And to answer your question, I don't think we would still be together. Some lies are just impossible to get past, and if it wasn't the affair, it would've been about something else."

Emery's eyes widen, and I swear she looks like she might cry right here in my office at any second. Shit. I knew that I was bad at this, but I can't be this bad. I'm apologizing for fuck's sake.

"You don't owe me any information," Emery says. "I shouldn't have asked."

"But I'm glad you did," I say. "Fuck, I'm glad for everything from last night and this morning. Even if I shouldn't be."

Both of her eyebrows shoot up. "What does that mean?"

I sigh. I'm ruining this, completely. I run my hand through my hair and then look at her, directly.

She's so beautiful, even in the fluorescent light of my office. And the way she's looking at me, like she's counting on me to say the right thing, erases all of my doubts from earlier. In one moment, I decide I don't care about my concerns. Not a single one of them.

"I want more time with you," I tell her. "I know this is more complicated than it should be. I know it's dangerous. But I'm not done after one night. Are you?"

She bites her lip again, blinking those long lashes at me. Her lipstick's faded completely from earlier, but her lips are still so full. I can't help remembering the way they felt against my mouth, my cock. I want her, every inch of her, and there's no point in denying it.

"No," she whispers. "I'm not."

"Come here," I motion with my fingers, beckoning her to me where I'm perched on the edge of my desk. I pluck the coffee cup out of her hand with a grin, and once I've placed it safely out of harm's way I tug her into my arms. In less than a minute I've flipped her around so that she's sitting on my desk, her legs wrapped around my waist with her skirt pushed all the way up to her waist. She moans against my mouth as my hand reaches under her blouse and tweaks her nipple, rolling the already hard flesh between my thumb and forefinger. She moves forward on the desk and I press closer so that she can feel the hardness of my cock through my trousers. I run kisses from her mouth to her jaw and she whimpers, and fuck, I could do this all day.

"Not—here," she whispers suddenly, her voice nearly a shudder next to my ear.

I pull back to look at her.

"I can lock the door," I tell her.

"No," she whispers. "Someone… We shouldn't."

I smirk. "What happened to jumping me in the copy room?"

She pants a little. "I just think we should be more careful. Like you said, this is dangerous."

I nip at her ear. "Maybe I like the danger."

She smiles, a lingering look at my lips. "People will notice if I'm always disappearing in here."

She's right, of course. And she's looking out for me, which I appreciate.

"The conference, then," I say. "A full week away with me in Sun Valley. What do you say?"

She blinks. "The conference thing was real?"

Not completely, I want to admit, but real enough. Maybe

Ramon is right. Maybe Emery is the perfect person for the job. Besides, I need to be alone with her if I'm going to sort any of this out and away from the prying eyes of my own employees.

"It is," I say. "People like to call it the 'billionaires conference.' I'm going to need you to be my eyes and ears. Among other things."

She runs a playful fingertip along the outline of my cock. "I can only imagine."

"I thought you said not here," I say.

"Well," she says, now circling that infuriating finger. "Maybe just a tease."

I catch her wrist in my hand. "Are you trying to send me to my afternoon meetings with blue balls?"

She smiles and presses a chaste kiss to my lips, letting her hand drop. "Fine. I'll stop."

"But the conference," I press on. "You'll go?"

She nods. "Of course."

We both adjust ourselves so that she can leave the office without anyone suspecting anything between us. I write down the information for the conference out for her and hand it to her on a sticky note, giving her clear evidence of a professional—not personal—rendezvous. Then, she smiles and leaves me to my thoughts.

I know I'm making the wrong choices. I can see the red flags waving like a bull in front of a matador. But I tell myself that, at some point, it will be enough. This will end, and it will be an amicable end. She'll return to her life, and I'll return to mine.

But in the meantime, what could be so wrong about a little fun?

CHAPTER TWENTY-ONE

FOR THE REST of the week, I do my best to focus on my work. It isn't easy, especially now that Emery's refusing to do anything vaguely resembling hooking up at the office. It seemed playful that first day, a little bit of teasing that actually made the anticipation of another encounter hotter. But now, something's off.

It's not that she's being hostile or even chilly to me. She's friendly enough and even bats her eyes at me occasionally. But it's only occasionally, and honestly, she seems about as friendly with me as she does with everyone else. Including Ramon.

Ramon was thrilled when I told him that I'd changed my mind about taking Emery to the conference. He asked if he could do some work with her on the marketing to get her up to speed. I nearly offered to do it myself, but then I remembered that I am the CEO. It's my name on the company. I don't have the time—and shouldn't be acting like I have the time—to prep an intern for a conference. So all I could do was say yes.

And oh, she's perfectly pleasant with Ramon and Sandy as they do their prep together. I've only sat in momentarily on meetings between the three, but I've watched as she oohs and ahhs over the framed pictures of his kids in his office. She asks all the right questions. She's got her notes. She's thoughtful. She took the time to teach Sandy a few spreadsheet tricks, something that Sandy mentions nearly every single time she brings me a coffee now.

"That girl is so sweet," Sandy said just this morning. "She's got such a good head on her shoulders."

She gave me a pointed look before she left. I did not appreciate it.

But the point is that Ramon was right. She'll be great on this trip, and if she is as great as we all think she will be, she might even have found a place for herself beyond intern. As her boss, I should be thrilled. Especially since, with all the fawning those two are doing, no one could doubt I promoted her just because we hooked up—not that anyone knows that, thankfully.

But I'm not thrilled.

Instead, I'm wondering why she's treating everyone the same way she treats me. None of them made her scream with pleasure as they fucked her. None of them have seen the way her head tilts back as she moans and squeals with delight. And, perhaps more infuriatingly, none of them opened up to her about anything personal. At least, I don't think Ramon's confessing his marital problems to her. Not that he has any.

It's not that she's being cool, exactly. It's something else. Is it guilt? She only answers one out of every three text messages that I send her. Which is...annoying as fuck. She dodges anything too flirty on text, the closest she gets to flirting back is the occasional winking face emoji when I bring up the trip. It must be some Gen Z bullshit that I don't understand. That, or she's lost interest, but I don't believe that. Every now and again, I find her doe eyes on me, dipping to my abs or below, a flush covering her skin. I'll see her bite those pouty lips, and I know she'd be wet for me.

And I know she's new to the sex thing, but surely she gets that it was great between us, right? She can't think she can replace me with just any asshole and have it be the same. I'm not sure why I expect her to know that without any frame of reference in lovers. Yet the idea of her having a frame of reference in lovers so that she can appreciate how well I make her come infuriates me. Fucked if I do, fucked if I don't. Or something like that.

But I'm playing nice, even if I leave the office every day infuriated. After all, I'm not the kind of guy who throws himself at women. They come to me. And Emery Mills should be no different.

On the Thursday before the trip, I decide I can't stand it anymore. I have to get to the bottom of this. After all, it can't be anything that I've done. I've been nothing but a gentleman. I'm about ready to storm over to her cubicle and demand to know what's wrong when I get my first clue from Sandy.

"That girl," she says, shaking her head. "Such a sweetheart."

"Yes," I say, resisting the urge to roll my eyes. I'm used to Sandy's flattery of Emery by now.

"You know, she was asking me how to book the flight for this weekend," Sandy continues. "She was saying that she's been watching Expedia for cheap flights, but she wanted to make sure she had the schedule right so that she didn't miss anything."

My head snaps up. "She was trying to book a flight? Surely someone told her that she wouldn't need to."

Sandy laughs. "I told her she'll be taking the private plane with you, and she didn't believe me. She said she couldn't 'impose' like that. I really enjoy her Midwest manners."

"But you told her that it's not a choice?" I ask, my voice firm.

Sandy waves a hand. "Of course. And she accepted.

Honestly, I think she was relieved. I get the feeling that she might be having some financial struggles, you know? New York is expensive for anyone, let alone interns."

Alarm bells ring in my head. I remember Emery's face on the steps and her expression after seeing her phone the other day. Could it be those damn student loans that she mentioned that have been causing this problem?

I make the decision quickly. It's been said of me that I never sit on a decision for too long. I believe that business is as much a game of the mind as anything, and I trust mine to have strong instincts at this point. I pick up the phone and ask Sandy to come into my office, and then I ask her for two pieces of information. She blinks a little at first, not understanding what I'm asking for, so I repeat myself. Sandy's a pro though, so she keeps her thoughts to herself and returns with the information in her normal timely fashion.

The first task is simple, if annoying. It requires me being on hold for some time. How people deal with that, I don't know. Then it requires arguing. Normally, something this annoying I would pass off on Sandy, but the information is too personal. It would raise uncomfortable questions, so I do it myself. I'm transferred a few times—again, unsure how anyone deals with this. Finally I get what I want. Unbelievable that sending money should be this difficult. It's an hour of my life that I won't get back, but at least I feel like I've made progress. If there's one thing I can't stand, it's standing still.

The next task is easier and wrapped up in five minutes. It's a Band-Aid solution but one that will work for now.

There, I think, full of male satisfaction. *Now, I've taken care of everything.*

It takes less than an hour for Emery to knock on my office door. She enters with her eyes even wider than usual. She looks curious, if not concerned. Like she thinks someone's playing a trick on her.

"Mr. Duke," she says after I wave her in. "May I interrupt you?"

I nod. "Yes, of course. How can I help you?"

She shifts on her feet. I know the question she wants to ask me. But I won't ask it for her. Instead, I level my gaze at her, hoping I seem patient and open.

"I just got an alert," she says. "From my bank."

I stare back at her, the picture of innocence. "Is there a problem?"

She shakes her head. "No. But...but it seems that someone paid off my student loans. All of them."

"How generous," I say.

"Mr. Duke," Emery steps farther into my office. "Did...did you do this? Because you're literally the only person I know with the resources to do something like this." She shakes her head even as the words leave her mouth. "I feel ridiculous asking. Why would you pay off my debt. Why?"

For a moment, I just look at her. She's in a pink dress that hugs her curves perfectly. Her hair up and away so that I can see her eyes, one lone brown wisp falling across her cheek as she's focused on me. Sparkling a little in the light of my window.

"Yes, Emery," I admit. "I did."

Her mouth drops open. "But why? It was over $50,000."

"I wanted you to be able to focus."

She stares at me, her gaze a bit narrowed. "What do you mean?"

I look at her and gesture for her to sit down across from me. I want it to be clear to her that I've done this as a business move. One, because I have. Two, because if she takes it another way and is offended, I can insist on the business aspect. Three, because I need to convince myself that that's why I did it and not because I have feelings for the girl. Feelings are dangerous. Feelings cannot be fucked away.

This all feels very logical, really.

"This conference is a really big deal and the deal on the line with Pink is worth a lot more than fifty grand to me. I've noticed how distracted you've been, and Sandy mentioned to me that you've been having financial challenges. If this was the distraction, well, now it's been eliminated. Problem solved."

Emery just stares at me. "Problem...solved."

"Well, isn't it?" I ask, trying not to sound too frustrated. "You had this hanging over your head, and I took care of it, and now you can focus."

"On the conference," she says, her voice dry and her eyes narrowed.

"Yes, on the conference," I say. "Because it's an important deal."

Emery laughs, catching me off guard. She shakes her head, her eyes still narrowed as she looks at me. She looks fiercer than I've seen her before. There's a spark of the passion from when she called me out at the charity event.

"You're unbelievable," she says. "You didn't think that, oh, maybe I should *ask* what was going on with me? You thought you'd just do this and that I'd be like, oh, okay, now that all of my debt is taken care of, I can focus? And I thought you said you hated lying."

"I do. Hate lying," I grit out. "And how could I have asked you what was going on when you've been avoiding me, Emery."

That stills her, something conflicted passing across her face. But then she takes in a breath and levels me with another glare.

"I have been trying to protect you," she says. "You warned me—"

"Let me make it very clear to you," I say, standing to lean across the desk. "I don't need a little girl from Kansas to protect me. I take care of myself."

"Well, so do I!" Emery says, nearly shouting as she

straightens to her full height to meet me. We're nearly nose to nose now, both of us steaming with anger. Anger or, it's possible, something else.

"I didn't need you to do that," she says, biting out the words. "I had a plan. I was going to pay them off. And now I owe you."

"And that's a problem?"

She breathes hard. "Of course it is."

The moment's quick. In one movement, she's leaned over the desk and closed the inches between us. Our mouths come together in a frenzy of kissing, hard and desperate with each of us trying to take more from the other. In a moment, I've pulled her forward to my side and hiked up her dress. She's pawing at my shirt with impatient hands, fumbling with my buttons until she gets enough undone that she can pull it free. Then, my mouth's on her neck, tracing nips and kisses as she moans and presses against me.

"Touch me," she begs. "Please. Now."

I don't need to be asked again. In a moment, my hands are under her skirt. Rubbing the sensitive skin through the lace of her panties. She pants against me as my kisses dip lower to her collarbone.

"Now," she insists. "Can we? I need you right this second."

I press another kiss to the hollow of her throat as I slip my finger under her panties and find her wet for me. She's soaked, and I wonder if this want was building from the moment she walked in my door. I feel the vibration of the moan in her throat as I plunge inside of her with a finger, relishing the feel of her tightening around me. It's been too long since I was inside of her, and we both know it.

"More," she begs. "God, Harrison, I want you to fuck me right here. I know we should be good but—"

She cuts herself off, her hands moving to my belt, impatient and fumbling as she continues to buck against my hand.

Her fingers brush against my hard cock as it strains against my trousers, eager to be free.

Eventually, I'm forced to stop fucking her with my hand so that I can push down my pants, letting my cock spring free between us. Emery immediately wraps her hand around it, reverently stroking it up and down as I groan.

Her eyes find mine, full of lust, as she scoots closer to the edge of the desk, her legs parted and ready for me.

Her hand continues its stroking as I reach into my wallet for a condom. A condom I've verified is there more times than I care to admit, waiting on this exact moment to present itself like a goddamned teenager. Emery watches hungrily as I rip open the packet, removing her hand so that I can slide it on. Then I lean forward and run a trail of kisses along her jaw before catching her mouth again in mine.

"Tell me again," I demand. "Tell me what you want."

"I want you to fuck me right here," she says. "On your desk," she adds, with a coy little laugh, as if she's amused to have found herself here.

I drive into her with a deep stroke as she arches her back and moans, grinding her hips forward to take more of me. I force myself to take it slow, remembering how new she is to this, but she only wants more. She braces herself back on her elbows, tilting her hips up, allowing me to press deeper and deeper into her until we're both groaning in satisfaction. Until I'm buried so deep inside of her, so wet and tight, I nearly embarrass myself by blowing my load before she's there with me. I hold on until she comes, biting her lip to keep from letting out the scream that I know she wants to emit. The sight is so hot, with her hair loose and wild from her earlier bun and her face flushed with her orgasm. I hold on for three more strokes, my orgasm rocketing through me as I spill into her, my own body shaking.

We sit there for a moment, both of us breathing hard from

the exertion. I help her sit up so that we're cheek to cheek, me still inside of her, her legs wrapped around me.

"So we have one full week of this at the conference," she says in a ragged voice.

"Yes," I answer.

"Then we better make the most of it," she says, pulling me into a kiss.

Danger, the alarm bells in my mind blare. *Danger ahead.* An affair with an intern is a stupid idea. She'll get hurt and my reputation will take a hit.

But I don't care. Not now, still inside her, with her heart beating so close to mine and her head resting on my shoulder.

Fuck danger. Fuck all of it.

CHAPTER TWENTY-TWO

"AND WE'RE the only ones on the plane? Like, it's just us?"

Emery's in my apartment, once again in my robe, a suitcase open in the corner. Since we'll be at the conference, I decided we needed to upgrade her wardrobe. But I don't have her pull from Blythe's hand-me-downs. This time, I've hired a stylist to select a variety of styles for her to choose from. They're arranged on racks around the living room, and Emery's been taking her time working her way through them to select what she wants to pack. She'll pull on a skirt and a top to model for me as I sit back in one of my leather chairs, and depending on how I react—usually by resisting the urge to rip it off of her—she decides whether or not to keep it.

"It's a private plane," I say, chuckling. "That's what the 'private' part means."

"I haven't flown much," she says. "My last flight was the one that took me from Kansas to New York."

"And did you enjoy the experience?"

She scrunches her nose. "Not really. I was sitting next to this guy who smelled like he'd just smoked a pack of cigars. He kept wanting to talk to me about New York, too."

"I thought you loved talking about New York," I say.

"Not with a man I don't know who smells like a chimney stack," she says. "Anyway, I think the experience will be much better this time around."

"Did he hit on you?" I ask, because great. I'm that guy now.

"Really?" she pauses in the act of folding something into the suitcase to arch a brow in my direction. "You want to know if some random dude, that I described as stinky, from a flight I took weeks ago, hit on me?"

I shrug, not attempting to hide my smile. I like when she sasses my ridiculousness.

"Are you nearly ready," I ask, checking my watch. "Have you packed everything you'll need?"

She thinks about it. "I hope so. And hopefully I'll look like a professional grown-up, who is wearing her own clothes."

"They are your clothes," I remind her.

She tucks a folded blazer into the suitcase. "That you bought me."

"Gifts. Which make them yours. Besides they're necessary for the trip, it's the least I could do."

"So you buy clothes for all of your employees?" she shoots back, a teasing grin on her face because we've had this... debate already.

"I think Leo is here," I respond. It's a deflection because teasing tone or not, there's no point in getting into an argument with a woman if it can be avoided.

"All right then." Emery snaps the suitcase closed with a dramatic flourish, flashing me a cheeky grin. "I'm ready for the billionaire conference!" But her smile of satisfaction only lasts a moment before a look of doubt replaces it. "Wait. Am I ready for a billionaire conference? How could I possibly be ready to attend a conference with a bunch of billionaires? Hi, my name is Emery, I'm a thousandaire," she deadpans. "Nice to meet you. Please take me and my twelve hundred dollar net worth seriously."

"For starters, no one introduces themselves with their net worth," I assure her, trying not to laugh. "And secondly, they're not all billionaires, and the ones that are…well, most of them will only be thinking of themselves."

"You're not like that," she says.

I shrug. "Or maybe I am."

She walks over to me and straddles me as she kisses me. "Nope. I'd know it if that was true."

I laugh. "You're trying to make us late again."

Eventually, I manage to get us out the door, though letting Emery get dressed is a task in self-restraint. Leo slides our suitcases into the trunk, smiling knowingly as he does though thankfully not saying a word. Then, we're off to Teterboro, with Emery pressed against me in the car. After last night in the office, she hasn't left my side. I haven't spent this many consecutive hours with someone since I was married, and even then, it's been years—if ever—since Blythe and I were joined at the hip. Yet, I find that I'm enjoying having Emery in my space. Clothes and dirty dishes, aside. It feels nice having her around, and like I'd miss her if she wasn't there. Which is… I brush those thoughts aside and focus on the business of the trip.

"Have you been studying?" I ask her.

"When would I have had time to do that?" Emery asks, winking up at me and reminding me of how we spent the evening tangled up in each other. "Just kidding. Yes, I spent all of last week getting ready. Go ahead. Quiz me. I dare you."

I do, and I don't leave anything out. I quiz her on every known competition we could possibly encounter—particularly the ones I suspect might be trying to poach Pink—and on the general schedule for the conference. I also quiz her on general business strategy and communication, but she doesn't even bat an eye and passes through those questions easily.

"Why are you only an intern?" I ask, genuinely curious. "Sandy was right. You do pick things up quickly."

She just shrugs. "Everyone has to start somewhere, right?"

I haven't thought about starting somewhere in such a long time. Fresh starts are a young man's game and I've been in this business for so long that all I can think about is the next project, the next get. But for Emery, her journey—wherever it may take her—is just beginning. The thought makes me uncomfortable, so I push it aside.

Once we're at the airport, we board my Gulfstream. Emery's eyes widen when we step onboard, her lips quirked in awed amusement. The interior of the main cabin is full of warm, creamy leather with white and black trim, generous sized seats along one side that each come with their own ottoman for resting tired feet. Along the other side is a TV that takes up most of the wall, and luxurious leather compartments for storing carry-on luggage. In the back, there's a bedroom and a full bathroom, along with a galley kitchen where the flight attendant is already busily prepping.

"This is insane," Emery says.

"And you wanted to fly coach." I smirk.

She gives me a smile, but it's a slightly strained one. I wonder if this is uncomfortable for her. I remember her comments at the charity event and her critique of my life of excess. But then she's walking over to one of the chairs and dropping down into it, exploring the buttons on the armrest.

"Holy cow," she says. "Does this chair have a back massager in it?"

I nod. "Of course. I couldn't do a flight without it."

"Mm," she purrs. "I suppose I could get used to this."

As the plane takes off, Emery spins in her chair to watch as we roar down the runway and then ascend into the sky. She watches each passing cloud with glee, her expression's completely free and unguarded. My mind drifts back to when Blythe used to be in that chair, permanently glued to her laptop or her phone. I know it isn't healthy for me to compare them, but in moments like this, it's hard not to.

It's still early by the time we're at cruising altitude, and the flight attendant brings out plates of raspberry French toast, flaky croissants, bowls of fresh fruit, and freshly squeezed juices. Emery devours it all, licking her fingers after some of the syrup drips down from her fork. Part of me wants to whisk her into the bedroom at the back, but I resist. Let her enjoy this experience. For me, it's another flight, but for her, this is a rare experience, one she isn't likely to repeat often.

Besides, banging her on the flight to a work conference reeks of a dickhead maneuver, doesn't it? This is temporary. I don't have to be a cliché bastard to top it all off.

Temporary.

Again, that twinge in my stomach reappears, but I tell myself it's only the rich pastries.

Eventually, Emery settles in with a book. It's a marketing book, no doubt recommended to her by Ramon. I can see by her bookmark that she's far in, and she turns the pages eagerly. She catches me watching and smiles. I'm charmed that she's reading a paper copy, and when she whips out a highlighter I mentally re-evaluate why we're not making use of that bedroom.

Towards the middle of the flight, I step into the galley to make a call, checking in with Ramon one last time before the conference. He doesn't have any new information about the poaching situation, but he does tell me that, unfortunately, Blythe had to drop out at the last second and won't be attending.

I correct him. "You mean fortunately."

"Agreed. But I just wanted you to be aware. I think she's sending someone else, but I didn't catch who."

Days away with Emery with Blythe ten states away? Nothing could be better.

"Anyway," Ramon says, and I hear one of his kids shrieking in the background. To be fair, it might have been laughing but it sounded like a shriek to my child-free ears.

"Have fun. Emery's more than prepared, and I think she'll be a great asset to you."

Indeed. She is. She is.

"Thanks," I reply, fighting off the guilt over the number of ways Emery is an asset. "I'll check in with you later."

By the time I get back to my seat, Emery's passed out, asleep, her book spreadeagled on her lap. I grab it gingerly and tuck her bookmark in between the pages, watching as her chest rises and falls with each breath. She's so fucking pure that it hurts. Not an ounce of treachery or ulterior motives in this girl. She's an open book, as it were. Forthright and honest and painfully trusting.

The idea of her on her own in a city like New York causes my chest to tighten. Hell, the idea of her on her own in Kansas doesn't do much for me either.

Focus, Harrison, I tell myself. Business trip, with a side of pleasure. Not the other way around. Because, after this, the excitement will wear off. It has to.

But in the meantime, with her peacefully sleeping beside me, I can forget about that. Especially with the news that Blythe won't be lurking at the conference this week. Hallelujah. Part of me wonders why in the world she'd be missing it, but it's a part that's easily overpowered by the freedom this will allow.

Of course, not too much freedom. I still have to play it professional with Emery. No one, especially not this crowd, needs to know that I'm sleeping with an intern. The fucking field day these assholes would have.

Business and pleasure, I tell myself. *Co-existing just a little while longer.* How hard could it possibly be?

CHAPTER TWENTY-THREE

WE'RE MET at the airport by a car service. Minutes later, we're pulling up to the famous Sun Valley Resort, our car idling behind others headed for the same conference. Emery peeks through the window, watching as each car stops, doors opened by a valet. She identifies each guest as they exit their cars. She's definitely done her research.

"That's James Tyler," she says. "CEO of Paradigm. Net worth, 56 million. A relatively low player. And that's Marianne Cooper, CEO and founder of Cooper Industries. She's—"

"—one of the ones we need to be on the lookout for," I finish. "Yes, exactly."

I get a look at Marianne through the window over Emery's shoulder. She's in her mid-fifties with a short, severe-looking bob. She's in a power suit, clicking past a huddle of men in polos and shorts.

"Why do they all look so...casual?" Emery asks, following my line of vision.

"Some of these guys think they're too successful to dress like they are," I say. "They think the more billions they have, the slouchier and dumpier they're allowed to look. Trying to be the next Zuckerberg or Steve Jobs, I guess. Or perhaps, they think dressing like a frat boy makes them look younger, who the fuck knows."

Emery glances back at me, making a bit of a hum in her throat. "I prefer a suit, I believe."

Her eyes are pools of warm brown, and they dip down to where my cock twitches in my trousers at her compliment. Up front, the driver clears his throat.

"We're up next, Mr. Duke," he says.

Valets swarm the car, grabbing our luggage and opening our doors. One of them, a particularly eager kid, nearly trips over himself to take Emery's hand to help her out. She laughs, high and tinkling, and the smile he gives back to her is like someone who's been gifted the sun.

"Deliver these to my room," I tell him, thrusting a hundred into his hand. "Quickly."

He blinks and scurries off to make it happen, and Emery raises an eyebrow at me.

"I don't want to have to wait around," I tell her. "We have networking to do."

She just smiles, bobs her head in a quick nod, and follows me. The resort is spread out, made to look like a giant, expensive cabin set against a mountain backdrop. There are lush green grounds, and people whiz past us on bicycles. These people are, of course, fellow attendees. The resort was fully booked for this week's retreat, and no one without prior approval is allowed on the grounds. There are probably paparazzi waiting at the precise point that they're allowed to be, with their long lenses desperate to capture the comings and goings of the event's elites.

"Up this way," I tell Emery, placing my hand on her back before I remember where I am and how many eyes could be looking. Dropping my hand, I take a quick glance around. No one's paying us close attention, but everyone's doing the cursory glance of who's here. I spot a few that I recognize, but besides our earlier sighting of Marianne, no one that I need to stop and talk to is here yet.

"Let's check in," I say. "Over here."

It's easy to tell that every employee working today is well aware of the tip potential this conference will bring. Every smile is permanently planted on their faces, and their voices are just a little too high. I shift uncomfortably as we approach a young woman at the counter, her round face smiling eagerly.

"Welcome to Sun Valley, Idaho," she chirps. "We hope you had pleasant travels. Can I get you checked in?"

"Oh, sure," Emery says, cutting me off before I can say anything. "Um, Emery Mills?"

"And Harrison Duke," I say. "We're in separate rooms."

Emery glances at me. She knows that this is just for appearance's sake. I don't plan to let her out of my bedroom for any longer than necessary.

"Of course," she says. "Looks like the paperwork was taken care of in advance, so let me just get you your keys."

She slides one of those cardboard key envelopes to Emery, with, no doubt, a plastic key for a standard room. Then, she hands me mine, which I know contain keycards for a luxury suite.

"We hope you enjoy your stay," she says. "And please enjoy the complimentary gifts and let us know if anything is wrong with your suite, Mr. Duke."

She eyes me, a bit of hunger in her eyes. Emery isn't the only one who can turn a head here, apparently.

"Thank you," Emery says, turning me around. As we walk away, she hands me her key envelope.

"I won't be needing that, will I?" she asks, batting her eyelashes at me.

"No," I practically growl. "You most certainly will not need that."

We're about to work our way to the lobby when a big, booming voice cuts through the noise.

"Harrison Duke!" the voice calls out.

I turn and see a crowd of older men at the bar, one of them with a long beard. I recognize the man as Geoffrey Paulson, an associate that I've known since I first got into the business. He's got a drink in hand, probably a brandy unless things have changed, and he's waving me over to the group. I sigh. If I'm going to have to network, he's an easy place to start. He might also be able to give me some insight on the Pink situation since he's known to have fairly loose lips. Besides, he's harmless, and in a week filled with plenty of predators, he'll be a nice way to ease in.

"You go get settled," I tell Emery, slipping a key for my suite into her little cardboard envelope and passing it back to her. "I'm going to stop at the bar."

She nods. "Great. I'll be down in a bit." She gives me a small smile and then turns around, heading off to the golden elevators that aren't far off. I force myself to turn away from her and into the bar, where top shelf liquor's sloshing in crystal glasses.

"There you are," Geoffrey says. "Knew you'd be here. Was just telling the guys that I couldn't wait to catch up with world-famous Harrison Duke."

I try to smile. It's odd, how fake my own smiles feel to me when they're not directed at Emery. "It's good to see you, Geoff."

"We were all just talking," Geoffrey says, waving to the suits behind him who have turned into their own conversations. "And maybe you know more. Apparently, there's a new company on the block, and they're trying to poach clients from the rest of us."

That perks up my ears. Sounds like my problem with Pink might be a common one. But I keep my face neutral.

"Is that so?"

"Some new suit," Geoffrey says. "I haven't heard of him before, but apparently he's been in the business awhile, hopping from pond to pond. A guy named—"

A bout of raucous laughter at a section nearby cuts Geoffrey off. I turn and see a trio of businessmen chuckling and smirking together, their drinks nearly drained and their voices too loud. They're younger, probably low-level executives who were lucky enough to be chosen to come here, and there's a heavy cloud of cologne hanging over them.

"Look at her," one of them says, gesturing with his glass. "What I wouldn't give to get with her this week."

Something drops in my stomach because, instinctively, I know who they're talking about. I know who they've spotted. I follow their line of vision and see Emery still at the elevators, having once again run into the overeager valet. He's talking to her with very animated hands, and she's laughing at what must be a very stupid joke. She throws back her head and smiles, dazzling him again. They look like a matched pair, both similar ages, young and carefree and sticking out with their youthful optimism and wide-eyed excitement to be in the midst of this event. Not a drop of the boredom that is so de rigueur that it's nearly a requirement amongst my set.

Still, my loathing of the valet cannot compare to my loathing for the men near me.

"You think she'll fuck him?" one of them says, pointing at the valet with his glass.

Geoffrey has stopped talking. Maybe there's more rage showing on my usually neutral face than normal. But I don't care. I want to see what else these assholes have to say.

"Nah," another one says. "She's just flirting with him to get his dick hard. She's probably here to land a rich old fucker. Gold digger potential right there. I can just tell by her mouth. That's a girl willing to suck senior dick if the pre-nup has potential."

If it was possible to see the heat radiating off of me, I'd be drawing far too many eyes right now. I push back from the bar, nearly sending my drink crashing. I catch it with my hand before it spills and adjust my tie.

"Excuse me, Geoffrey," I say, not even looking at the man. "I forgot that I have an appointment."

I push past him and stride straight towards the men, not bothering to adjust my path as I get near them. They jump apart, their overpriced drinks sloshing onto the carpet.

"What the fuck?" one of them says, and then, no doubt recognizing me, his eyes go wide.

But I don't pause to make a scene, or give them a piece of my mind. I have some restraint left. An iota. Instead I keep going, striding straight for Emery and the valet. He sees me over her shoulder and mumbles something, stepping back from her as he stares at the floor.

I place my hand on her shoulder, and she spins to me, her eyes brightening at the sight of me.

"Harrison," she says. "I thought you had business."

"I have something else to do first," I say, then look pointedly at the valet.

"The bags are already in your room, sir," he says. "I'll just—"

I reach over and press the button to our floor, my eyes never leaving him.

"You'll be going," I finish for him, and he nods and scuttles away. My hand hasn't left Emery's shoulder, and she glances at it and raises an eyebrow.

"What happened to playing professional?" Emery says, lowering her voice to a whisper.

"No," I say. "They all need to know."

The elevator dings, opening before us. Emery glances at it.

"Know what?"

"That you're mine," I say, letting my hand drop to her waist. She leans into my touch and bites her lip.

The elevator doors have barely pressed shut before her mouth is on mine.

Her lips are soft, pliant, and eager against mine, and I gather her into my arms and hoist her against the wall of the elevator as her legs wrap themselves around my hips to hold on. Our mouths move hungrily against one another, our tongues seeking and darting and dancing together. My hands cup her ass, squeezing gently as I nip at her lower lip.

"You were jealous," she says, pulling back to kiss and whisper against my ear. "I can't believe you."

"Of course I was." I'm incredulous. "What man wouldn't be?"

She wraps her legs tighter around me, and I move one hand from holding her ass to cupping her breast. She arches against me, and I tweak her nipple through the thin fabric. She moans, her nipple hardening at my touch. I want her breasts in my mouth, and then I want to taste all of her and make her come again and again until she forgets about every other man who's dared to look at her.

"We're nearly to our floor," she pants, glancing at the lit-up lights.

"Then I'll pull the emergency break," I say, but she swats at me before I can.

"We're feet away from a perfectly good hotel room," she reminds me. "And besides, aren't you worried about someone seeing?"

No, is my first instinct. I want them to see. I want them to know that I'm the one she's with. I'm the one who gets to have her, who gets to give her pleasure and joy. I'm the one she looks for across a room. Me, and no one else.

But I can't say that. I sigh and let her down, her feet finding the floor. She doesn't push me back, though, and I don't make the move either. I stay flush against her, pressed so close that she can feel every throbbing inch of me. I want her to know how much I want her, how close I am to needing her. How easy it would be to push up her skirt and press inside her, because my want for her is unending, a constant ache.

She bites her lip and runs her hand along my jaw, leaning up so that her mouth is inches from mine.

"None of them," she whispers, the warm air brushing against my face. "None of them could ever compare to you, Harrison. You should know that. I want you to know that," she adds and her words are so pure, her tone so earnest, they cut me wide open.

Fuck, forget about privacy. Our room feels impossibly far away. Painfully far away. I kiss her again, hungrily, feverishly, and she kisses back, just as desperate.

The elevator dings, and we stop. Our breathing is ragged as we step apart. She straightens her hair, and I adjust my tie. Then, I look up to what I expect to be the empty floor.

Except that it isn't empty.

Claire is there.

And one look tells me that she might not have seen everything, but she certainly saw enough.

CHAPTER TWENTY-FOUR

"WHAT IN THE hell is wrong with you?"

It's a fair question, on an ordinary day. Let alone on the day you've just been caught making out on an elevator with an intern. Your intern. Your fresh out of college—oh fuck it. It's a good question, is the point.

I left Emery in my suite to shower and change—and to allow her some privacy to deal with the embarrassment of having been caught making out with me in an elevator—by the company lawyer of all people. Then I took Claire down to the room reserved for Emery, so we could have this out in privacy.

The fact that Claire is the one who caught us, in addition to being my legal counsel, in addition to being another employee that I've had sex with, well fuck.

I'm having a day, clearly.

Emery's room is a nice enough space but nothing compared to my suite upstairs. Not that it matters. How nice the décor is seems irrelevant when you're getting dressed down by your lawyer. And ex-lover. Let's not forget that bit of awkward.

"I saw you," she says. "All over each other as if there

aren't a thousand other people in this hotel, any one of them who would love to have a bit of torrid gossip on you, and on Duke Capital. Were you even trying to hide it?"

It's a sign of how much I fucked up that Claire isn't even trying to hold back. Normally, she would demur or sidestep, an acknowledgement that I'm the boss. She'd be subtle when she told me I was an asshole. But now? Now, she doesn't give a shit.

"I made a mistake," I say. "I didn't expect anyone to be up there, hovering around."

"I was waiting for you," she says, her tone clear that she doesn't care for my insinuation that she was hovering. "Blythe sent me in her place; there are a couple of high-profile charity board members scheduled to attend that I'm signing contracts with on behalf of Duke Capital. But that doesn't matter. The point is that I needed to talk to you about urgent business with your company, and what do I find? You making my life, our life, really, really complicated. I thought you were better than this, Harrison."

Anger bubbles up in me. "Better than what, exactly?"

She has the decency to blush. She's dressed more casually than she usually is at the office, like so many of the others here. Not casual as in she's wearing an ugly polo; she's in white jeans and a brightly colored blouse, one that hugs her figure perfectly. Paired with heels, her look is effortless casual executive. Her hair's slicked into a low neat knot, all the better to see every vein in her forehead that's popped out with her anger.

"Better than sleeping with your intern, Harrison," she says. "God, do you even know her name?"

"Watch what you're suggesting, Claire," I say. "Emery and I have been spending quite a bit of time together as of late. Should I have been more discreet? Of course. But she's an intelligent, grown woman, and I hardly see how this is any of your business. Nor do I see anything wrong with it."

Claire bites out a cold laugh. "Oh really? Then let me, as your legal adviser, spell it out for you. You might think she's an 'intelligent woman,' but to the rest of the world, this screams of a midlife crisis. And now you're the CEO who's willing to take advantage of vulnerable young employees. Or you're being played by the company slut. That's how this plays out, Harrison. Oh, and in case you need to be reminded, you're still *married*."

My chest puffs up, ready to retort and to let Claire know exactly where she can shove what she's saying. But then her words hit me. Of course, I had considered the hit that the company might take if this were to leak out. I knew I would be scolded for it, ribbed, snide comments would be made. But Claire's last words there about Emery, about her reputation. I hadn't considered that.

What happens to Emery once our affair is over? I think of the way those businessmen thought they could talk about her earlier. When they knew nothing about her except she was a beautiful, young woman waiting for an elevator. How will she be talked about once news of us gets out? When she's viewed as the girl that slept with the boss?

I sink onto the bed and breathe in through my nose, my fingers gripping the edge of the bedspread until the fabric bunches in my fists. I've fucked up. I've made a terrible mistake.

Claire sits next to me, legs crossed and foot bouncing in agitation. For a moment, we both just sit there, each of us stewing in our thoughts.

Claire speaks first.

"Who knows?"

I sigh. "No one. Ramon saw us once, but he thinks it was a one-time thing."

Claire's head whips to me. "You were fucking at work?"

"No," I say, too quickly. "He caught us, ah. Doing something similar to what you saw."

Claire groans. "Harrison, you're not making my life easy."

I stand up. "It's nothing. It ends now."

Claire raises an eyebrow, looking up at me. I can see disbelief written on every inch of her face, and fuck, we both know I'm lying.

"I'll show more discretion, is what I mean. No one will know. For her sake. I swear."

Claire sighs and stands up, tapping two fingertips against her temple.

"Why her, Harrison? You could have any woman in New York. Or, hell, any woman, almost anywhere. Why her?"

I look at Claire. It's a perfectly reasonable question. And it doesn't completely escape my attention that Claire is the woman I lost interest in once Emery came along. Not that we had anything deep, or exclusive. But still, I'm not such a dick that I can't imagine it's an added sting. Claire is far more appropriate for me. We have more in common, run in the same circles. We're closer in age and at similar places in our careers.

Yet, she never held my interest as more than a friend with benefits. I never thought of her as more, or much at all, really.

My mind drifts to Emery earlier, her lips smiling as she called me "devastatingly handsome." The memory doesn't help me with an answer to Claire's question, though. If anything, it complicates it.

"I don't know," I say, then "I don't know," again, with a shake of my head. "But I'll take care of it."

"You better," she says. "Especially now."

She goes to the minibar and pulls out a tiny bottle of whiskey and downs it in one gulp.

"Why especially now?" I ask.

She breathes out through her nose and steadies me with a look. It's the kind of look you give someone before you punch them in the gut, a look that says you're going to destroy them just a bit and you wish you weren't the one who had to do it.

"Someone is trying to steal Pink."

"Jesus Christ," I shake my head. "Does everyone know about that?" Everyone but me, apparently. Since I've been too busy dicking around with my intern.

"Who else knows?" she asks, momentarily surprised.

"Ramon. He got a tip. He's been looking into it."

She nods. "I'll compare notes with Ramon, but I found out who it is."

I sit up straighter. "Who is it? Marianne?"

"No," she says. "Worse. You aren't going to like it."

She digs into the minibar and tosses me a whiskey.

"Just tell me, Claire."

She shakes her head. "Trust me, you're going to need that."

I roll my eyes but swallow the liquor to appease her. It works its way through my throat, burning all the way down. It must be cheap as hell. Claire watches the whole time, and once I've swallowed it down, she leans back and begins.

"It's Robert," she says. "He's the one trying to steal Pink. But not just them. He's going after an entire list of your clients. Ones you can't afford to lose."

I roll my eyes. "Robert doesn't have his own company."

Claire nods. "He doesn't. But he's found someone rich and dumb enough to be his puppet, and he's convincing them to go after the right clients."

I shake my head. "That's impossible. Ramon said that Pink was considering another company because they understood women better than we do."

"That's one theory," she says. "But we don't know for sure. And besides, who knows what kind of team Robert is assembling. Maybe he's promising to throw more money at Pink. Something tells me he'll do whatever it takes to win them over."

"It'd be a waste of money," I say. I feel oddly relieved. Robert was never a great businessman. He was decent, smart, and, like his current partner, manipulative. But Robert was always short-sighted, and I don't see a chance in hell of him pulling this off.

"You know he's motivated," she says. "And I think he's feeling particularly greedy after what you did to him."

"What *I* did to him?" I say, nearly snarling. "That piece of shit—"

"I don't mean with that," Claire says in a rush. "I mean your threat about the charity."

"How do you know about that?"

Claire holds up her hands. "Remember, I'm your lawyer. It's my job to know everything."

Now, I can't help it. I stand up, ready to shout her down.

"So you knew that they were screwing this company with their shady bullshit?"

Claire folds her arms. "Of course I didn't. But it came out, yes, after your threat. Blythe mentioned it to me, actually. I do have to speak with her about company business, you know. She gave me an earful after your fight. She wanted to make her case about the charity, I think. But I've done my own checking and I agree they're problematic. And none of this would be happening if you'd allowed the legal team more leeway with Blythe's department to begin with."

I wave off that comment with a dismissive hand, because I know. I already fucking know that I allowed Blythe too much freedom to fuck me over. "So what did you tell her?"

Claire sighs. "Harrison, we don't have time to talk about this. I've got a meeting with a possible philanthropy client in ten minutes."

"Doing more of Blythe's dirty work?"

She glares at me. "I'm here on behalf of Duke Capital, not Blythe. But yes, since she runs your charity division I suppose I'm doing her dirty work, if that's how we're referring to charitable donations now. But I don't want to argue about it. I shouldn't even have told you anything, but lucky for you I don't have any attorney client privilege with Blythe, and for reasons unbeknownst to me, I actually like you. So, if you want to save Pink from Robert, then you need to get off your ass, stop fucking around with your intern, and get downstairs. Close the deal before anyone can."

She puts the empty whiskey on the dresser and heads for the door.

"And Harrison?" she says, tossing her hair over her shoulder to look at me. "Remember that if you don't want to be married anymore, you don't have to be. Sign the goddamned papers if you're so motivated."

CHAPTER TWENTY-FIVE

ONCE CLAIRE LEAVES, I splash some cold water on my face and try to think. Everything she just said swirls around in my head, but all I can see is Robert's smug face in Blythe's office. They're both terrible, but Robert might actually be the worst of them. And that's saying a lot, since Blythe was—is—my wife. Yet, after all he's taken from me, I find out that he's trying to take more.

Then there's Emery. I brought her here, and in doing so, I've exposed her to even more danger than I do at the office. Lecherous men ogling her is bad, but subjecting her to bull-shit rumors is another thing entirely. And for what? To appease my own fucking ego? No. I should've listened to Ramon. I should listen to Claire. I should grab my things and stay in here, let Emery have the suite. I should stop this before it goes any further.

I've made up my mind. I head to the elevator and head up to the suite, my intentions set. I'm more careful exiting the elevator this time, wondering if Claire's come up here to scold Emery. The thought fills me with rage, but Claire's nowhere to be found. I let myself into the room, and as soon as I cross the threshold, I see her.

She's standing at the glass doors that look out over the mountain view, wearing a long, creamy dress made of some kind of gauzy fabric. There must be threads of gold sewn in, because it glitters a bit in the sunlight from outside. I'm sure I saw it back in New York when she packed, but as I walk to her and she turns her head to look at me she's haloed in the light.

Fuck. She's beautiful.

"Harrison," she says, her voice nearly a whisper. "I'm so sorry. I had no idea—"

I've crossed the room and pulled her into my arms before she can finish. Her kiss is soft but pleading, leftover from what we didn't get to finish in the elevator. But there's hesitation there, too, and it isn't hard to imagine why.

"You have nothing to be sorry about," I say after stepping slightly back. "I didn't even realize she was going to be here. Blythe sent her as a proxy."

At Blythe's name, Emery stiffens in my arms. She pulls away, turning back to the mountain view. I wish I knew what she was thinking. I wish I hadn't said Blythe's name at all. It's the ultimate mood killer, not that there was much left to kill after Claire saw us in that damn elevator.

"I'm the one who should be apologizing," I say. "All this time, I've only been thinking about the risk to my company. To me. I haven't been thinking about how this could impact you."

Emery looks back at me. "I think the problem is that you've only been thinking about me."

"No," I say. "Putting your reputation on the line like that…it wasn't right."

She steps towards me. "My reputation is my business, Harrison."

Those doe eyes are sparkling in the light again, and with each step she takes back to me, I feel my resolve crumbling. I know this is wrong. Inappropriate doesn't even begin to cover it. My lawyer just spelled it out for me, didn't she? I'm defiling the girl, again and again.

But doesn't she have a right to decide? It's a selfish question, one born because it fits the narrative that I want. The one that allows this not to end. But I don't care.

She's right here in front of me, her lips hovering just below mine. She wants this as much as I do, right or wrong.

And if she's choosing this, then I can at least make it worth her while.

"Bed," I tell her in a husky voice.

She bites her lip. "Harrison—"

With a deft finger, I reach under the flowy fabric of her dress and find her pussy wet through her panties. She gasps at the touch, light against the lace there, and presses forward, grinding gently against my finger.

"I need a taste, Emery," I say. "I need you."

On the last word, I slip my finger beneath her panties, delving between the soft lips there. I slip a finger into her and she clenches around me immediately, pushing forward and inviting me deeper, silently asking for more. I thrust my finger slowly, massaging her clit with my thumb as I do. She shudders against me, unable to speak as I trace kisses down her neck.

"Don't you want to give me just a little taste?" I ask her as I kiss near her ear. "Because I want you. Now."

"Y-yes," she manages to get out. "Oh, God, yes."

I push her back gently on the bed, and she collapses, legs dangling before me as I drop to the floor in front of her. I slide her panties over her hips and toss them aside, and then there she is, delicious and waiting for me. I flatten my tongue and run it through her center, reveling in the taste of her. Have I ever enjoyed going down on a woman as much as I enjoy it on Emery? Doubtful. She elicits some kind of caveman bullshit in me, one in which I want to mark her and lick her. Taste every inch of her. She tastes perfect, like fucking honey. I lick and tease and circle her opening with the tip of my tongue as she moans, her thighs quivering and her toes curling before I've barely gotten started. I hunger for her, with the need of a man who knows how much he's taken. With every nip and lick and slip of my tongue in just the right place, I try to give back, to make this moment, at least, one that will be worth all of the trouble I've caused her.

"Harrison," she moans. "Oh—" She fists her hand into my hair, keeping my head exactly where she wants it and I love it. I love knowing I'm the one who's shown her what she likes. I'm the one who's given her this confidence in bed, the ability to ask for what she wants, even if she's doing it unknowingly with a firm grip on the back of my head.

And my name on her lips? Magic. I respond by giving her what she wants, dipping my tongue inside of her, rimming her entrance, sucking and flicking her clit. Repeat. She shivers and writhes and I can feel the orgasm building in her, the one that I've brought, and I flatten my tongue and lick through her core before sucking her clit with enough force that her hips buck forward and she cries out my name, that hand in my hair tightening to a nearly painful grip as the other grabs a fistful of bedding as she rides over the edge.

My cock is hard in my pants, aching to be inside of her, but my own needs will wait. Now is about her and her alone, and as she continues to pant on the bed, I sit up and push her dress up further until I can gently tug it over her head. She's naked beneath it, no bra to be found, and the sight of her breasts heaving just slightly, her nipples hard as diamonds, sends fresh throbbing to my cock. I trace kisses from her shaking thighs to her stomach, then swirl my tongue around each nipple as she murmurs unintelligible cries of pleasure. I press a kiss to her neck that sends her shaking again, and that's how I know she's primed for more.

Two fingers into her swollen pussy, and she bucks her hips, grinding against them immediately, still riding the high of the first orgasm but ready and willing for more. And I'm just the man to give them to her. The only man to give them to her.

I continue to circle her nipple with my tongue as I thrust my fingers in and out, and then I nip her with my teeth. Just enough to cause a small bite of pain. Enough to surprise her, causing her to gasp, before I suck her tit in my mouth, sucking to match the beat of each thrust of my fingers. Her moan is feral, and her hands tug wherever she can reach. My shoulders, the bedding, her own neck at one point.

"Oh—oh—"

But those are the only words she gets out. I leave her swollen breasts and travel back down to her pussy, and when I plunge my tongue back in, her body responds with more shivers and shakes. The second orgasm takes no time at all. She's already there, ready for it to crash over her, and it's just a few flicks of my tongue before she's screaming my name again.

I lift my head to look at her as she breathes, her hand on her breast, her eyes closed and lips parted, pink and flushed with my kisses. The light of the window falls across her in a single beam of mountain light, and she is the most beautiful thing I have ever seen in that moment. In any moment.

I rise up on my feet and move so that I'm resting beside her. She tilts her head to look at me, still breathing hard.

"I didn't know I could… That was…"

I smirk, a cocky bastard through and through. "Oh, that's only the beginning."

Her eyes widen. "You're kidding."

"I never kid," I tell her. "If you're willing to face some fire for me, then you deserve at least four orgasms before dinner."

"Four?" Emery says, her eyes wide. "Before dinner?

Surely that's…impossible." But even as she says it her pupils dilate, her gaze lustful with a hint of curious.

I nip at her earlobe. "Are you ready to begin?"

The kiss she presses to my lips tells me all that I need to know.

CHAPTER TWENTY-SIX

WE SPEND the rest of the evening finding new ways to please each other, losing ourselves in each other's bodies. It's enough to temporarily push all of my concerns out of my mind, but once the sun's completely down and Emery's cleaning up in the bathroom, they resurface. I find myself staring out at the mountains that Emery was admiring earlier, wondering if they hold any answers. But of course, they're cold and indifferent. In some way, I can relate.

"We should talk about it," Emery says from behind me.

She's back in her dress after having ironed out the wrinkles I caused earlier. She's redone her hair in a braided sort of updo and added long earrings that brush the tops of her shoulders. If I didn't know better, I might not know that she's a girl from Kansas. She might be a girl from New York or Los Angeles, a young but powerful executive in her own right, or at the very least a Manhattan girl with a trust fund. Someone with a safety net, someone used to moving in these circles and knowing how to get what they want. But then she smiles at me, soft with those perfect lips, and her innocence and charm erase everything else. Her eyes are so damn guileless, she'll never pass for a jaded New Yorker.

"Talk about what?" I ask.

"About what Claire said to you," she says.

"I don't care," I reply, a bit dismissively, because I don't. "We'll be more discreet. But I'm not letting my lawyer boss me around. It's my company. My life. We'll be adults about it, and that's all there is to it."

Emery nods, biting her lip. "Right."

I rub my temple, the mention of Claire bringing up her other concerns.

"There is some news she told me that you should know," I say. "The person who's going after Pink is…"

Even though she knows about Robert, I hesitate to say his name. I don't need him spoiling this moment.

"He's here," I finish instead. "And trying to poach several of my clients, apparently."

Emery considers this. "Well, that's not new. We expected them to be here, didn't we? So the plan is the same: find out whatever we can on them and then use it to make sure Monica stays firmly on Team Duke, right?"

I laugh a little at "Team Duke," my mind straying to some very kinky team-building exercises I could do with Emery, but I tuck those thoughts away for later and nod. "True."

"What do you think their strategy will be?" Emery asks, eyes lighting up as she goes straight into the girl that has prepped so extensively for this conference.

"Not exactly sure," I say. "But I know the guy, and I have a feeling it'll just be to throw money at them."

"Can't we do that?"

I raise an eyebrow at her. "What do you think?"

She thinks about it, pacing in the room. "It'll need to be more. Monica will want something personal. We should have a dinner with her. Tonight. I think she's here with her wife."

"I think it's a bit late for that," I say, glancing out of the window.

"Then drinks," she says. "But we have to try. After all, this is your business, right? And no one plays this game better than you. Let's get our woo on."

There's fire in her words that ignites me, even as I fight back a smile at her usage of *woo*. She believes in me. And who gives a fuck about Robert? This is my client.

"You're right," I say. "I'll make the call."

When I call Monica, she's still in her room, recuperating from the trip. She sounds intrigued but not entirely surprised by my call. She must know that word's gotten around about her being poached. She agrees to meet me and my "associate" for drinks in the hotel's lounge, saying they'll be ready in fifteen minutes.

"It's a sign," Emery says. "I told you she'd want to."

"Luck is not a sign," I tell her.

"I disagree," she says. "Back on the farm, there were always signs that told me when I'd have a good day. And, of course, signs when it was going to be a very a bad day, but"— she waves her hand—"pffft."

"How does that work?" I chuckle. "You just rejected the signs you didn't like?"

She winks at me. "No. Of course not. I just took those signs as opportunities. Say I wake up and one of our crops is dying. Well, I took it as a lesson and made sure the other crops were properly tended to. Research, see if there's anything to be done to save the ones in distress, Then, voila! The message of the day isn't lost revenue on the bad crops. It's that all the others got some extra TLC."

I shake my head. "That doesn't make any sense."

"You'll see, Mr. Duke," she says with a wink. "This is going to be a great night."

We meet Monica in the lounge and find her and her wife seated in a booth far in the back. It's lit with low, warm lighting, but the corner's dark and separate. She knows this is a conversation we'd rather others not hear.

We're on the same page, there.

"Monica," I say. "It's nice to see you again."

"And to see both of you," she says, smiling as she shakes Emery's and my hands before gesturing to the red-haired woman next to her. "This is my wife, Tatiana."

"Nice to meet you," Emery says.

We get through the pleasantries first as we order our drinks. We talk about the travel in, and Emery gushes about the beauty of Idaho, the lushness of the resort and her general excitement.

Monica laughs, clearly enchanted by Emery's charm.

"And we get more time with you," Emery continues. "I'm just so thrilled you could meet with us tonight. Pink is such a fantastic opportunity."

Monica smiles, but Tatiana raises an eyebrow.

"And what is your...opportunity?" Tatiana asks. "I'm sorry. What's your role at Duke?"

"Oh," Emery says, blushing. "I'm an intern, for now. I'm helping out wherever they need me."

"Emery has been a great asset," I say. "We all have to start somewhere, and we do our best to develop new talent at Duke Capital. To provide opportunities from within, even as we work to partner with clients for which we can do the same. I'm sure you can appreciate that."

That's basically true. We have interns.

"So you're helping him acquire new business?" Tatiana asks. Monica's eyes cut to her in a warning glare.

"I help wherever I'm needed," Emery says, unfazed. "I believe in Duke Capital. I've seen how they listen and really care about the clients they take on. When you're new, when you're interviewing, you hear these horror stories about toxic work environments and businesses that just want to throw money around and not actually grow something. But at Duke...they really care. *Mr. Duke* really cares about his clients, and I've seen it firsthand. It's something special."

Her eyes flash to mine, glittering. I sit back and sip my

whiskey, watching her. Does she really believe that? Or is it just part of a very well-done, subtle pitch? I guess I did listen to her about the charity, even if I haven't been able to do anything about it yet.

But suddenly, her words give me an idea.

"Actually, Emery helped me with an idea for Pink," I say. "If you're willing to hear it, I can talk through it right now. Especially since it might help with signing those contracts you've been holding on to."

Monica smiles innocently. "You know how long paper-work takes to handle."

"And we both know you're being courted by others," I say firmly. "So let me tell you why we're the way to go."

Monica leans back, sipping her wine as she gestures for me to proceed.

"We know that your company is about creating a space for the female client," I say. "You want to make a site that's specifically for them and their interests, without judgement and without shame. And we support that, completely.

But what if you could do more?" I ask. "We have the financing and the experts—because it can't be just about money, can it? It has to be people who know what they're doing with your company, with your image and brand. And what if…" I pause, drawing her in. "Clearly your goal is to change the narrative on female sexuality. A shame-free site geared towards women. But what if you could make a real difference while doing so? A difference bigger than social acceptance?"

"I'm listening," Monica says.

"For every new subscriber," I continue. "A donation is made to a charity, ones that align with your values."

"Charities for porn?" Tatiana interjects, clearly doubtful of my agenda.

"No, charities for women. Charities that support birth control or sex education, perhaps. They don't need to be sexually based of course, they could be about helping women get back into the work force, or assisting women on leaving an abusive relationship. The donations would, of course, be funded completely by Duke Capital. Doing good while getting off. What could be better?"

I glance at Emery as her eyes light up, a small smile twisting her lips, her head nodding in agreement.

"Fully vetted charities, I add. Ones with low overhead that do the most good. Maybe we can even find a start-up charity, or a woman-run charity to spotlight. And we can put the choice in the consumers' hands. Let the subscribers pick which of our featured charities their subscription supports. Letting a woman choose is what Pink is all about, after all. Women embracing their own power. Think of all the good you could do."

I sit back, letting the idea rest on the table. I feel Emery straighten up next to me, and under the table, her hand finds my knee and squeezes it.

"And this was your idea?" Tatiana says, eyes sliding to Emery.

Emery bites her lip and smiles. "One of my intern rotations was with our charity department and it's something I'm passionate about. I've given Mr. Duke an earful on the subject, which he's been gracious enough to listen to. It's a bit personal for me, as my family benefitted greatly from charity when I was younger. My brother..." She pauses briefly, clearly not wanting to get too personal. "There were some organizations that made a big difference in his life, in our entire family's lives."

That shuts Tatiana up. She sits back and looks at Monica, who's still sipping her wine.

"It's interesting," Monica says. "I like it. And I like the idea of giving the customer the power to choose. And Duke Capital would be willing to provide this funding for the charities? At no extra charge to us?"

"Completely," I say. "Claire is here, I'll have her amend the contract tonight, and we can finalize the deal right here at this conference."

Monica exchanges a look with Tatiana, then beams and holds out her hand.

"Mr. Duke," she says. "I believe you have a deal."

CHAPTER TWENTY-SEVEN

FINALIZING the agreement with Pink makes the rest of the conference feel unnecessary, and a bit anticlimactic. And knowing Robert is here, lurking about puts a dent into any enjoyment I'd have being here with Emery. So we cut out early, heading back to New York the following evening. I make sure to squeeze in a couple of face-to-face meetings with clients that need to see me before we cut out. To subtly remind them what Duke Capital has done for them, and will continue to do. The experience and professionalism we've delivered. Let that be fresh on their minds when Robert slinks in with his sleezy pitches.

One of the many privileges of owning your own plane and keeping a pilot on standby is the ability to change your flight plans on a whim. Add in a late takeoff with an overnight flight and we'll be back in New York in the morning without even missing another day.

Claire has already amended the contract and sent it to the legal team in New York for final review. I've looped Ramon in and he's revising budgets and coordinating with the different departments involved at Duke to make my promises to Pink a reality. There's a lot to get done, a lot to coordinate, but Emery and I can sleep on the plane and hit the ground running in the morning.

She's giddy as we pack up, which honestly doesn't take long since we barely had any time to get unpacked in the first place. She keeps looking at me and grinning, occasionally shaking her head like she can't believe what she's seeing.

"You are incredible," she says at last, reaching over to pull me by my tie into a kiss, still reminiscing about our meeting with Pink. "I've never seen you like that. So...alpha."

I chuckle. "You were my inspiration."

She bites on her lip, her hand still on my tie. "That was such a genius move, adding the donations. I wouldn't have even thought it was possible, combining a business deal with charity. And by the way"—she gives my tie a tug along with a sexy grin—"charity is really sexy."

"Why not?" I ask. "I knew I had to do something creative to seal the deal with Pink. And it solves two issues as it were. I've been trying to figure something out with the charity issues you brought to my attention. My original donation was a start, but this is something long-term."

"What donation?" Emery asks, her grip loosening.

I take her hand. "I did something."

She blinks. "What is that?"

"I know it doesn't undo the mess with some of the charities Duke Capital is currently supporting, but I want to make it right. I know there's still more work to be done, but I made a donation to the charity you told me about. The one that helped your family. I matched the amount we donated to that sham of a charity and wrote another check."

For a moment, she just stares at me. Then, she steps back, shaking her head.

"But wasn't...didn't you already donate hundreds of thousands of dollars to them?"

"Close to a million," I say. "So I rounded up."

"Harrison, that's...that's..."

"I had to make it right," I say. "And if I couldn't pull those funds and reallocate them, then this was the next best thing. At least, I thought it was at the time."

It's her expression that worries me. She's still shaking her head, turned away from me. Is she incredulous? Or have I shamed her? Does she think I'm trying to buy her with something like this? First I pay off her student loans, then I make an enormous donation to a charity that is very personal to her. Maybe this isn't how normal men behave, how the fuck am I supposed to know?

"I'm sorry if I overstepped," I say. "I made it anonymously, if that helps."

She turns around, tears pooling in her eyes. They take me aback. I am not good with crying women in general, but a crying Emery? It feels like a punch to the gut. Like there's a shaky trapdoor beneath my feet.

"You," she whispers, "are nothing like what I expected, Harrison Duke. Not at all what I thought."

She presses herself into my arms, her cheek resting against my chest as she embraces me. I hold her there, unsure exactly what to do with her. This isn't sex, easily navigated. This is something more intimate, and it terrifies me.

"Is that a good thing?" I ask, trying for levity in my voice.

She pulls back and wipes at her eyes with her hands.

"Yes," she says with a laugh. "It is."

A buzz on the door tells us that the valet's here—hopefully not the same douche that checked us in—ready to take us to the plane. Emery grabs my hand and squeezes it.

"Thank you," she says. "For…everything."

All I can do is nod. I don't know what "everything" entails, and there's something sad about Emery's look. But she's already turned away, heading to open the door so the moment is lost. I need to get us on the plane, back to the office, and then work on sorting all of this out. I want the

feeling from earlier back. The celebration, the victory. The...
happiness. This new energy between us unnerves me.

She's quiet, even after we've pulled away from the hotel
and right up until the plane takes off. Once we're in the sky, I
tell her to go get some sleep, take advantage of the onboard
bedroom. She doesn't object, heading to the back of the plane,
and whether or not she wants me to follow her, I don't. I give
her some space, because I need to digest everything that's
happened over the last few days.

Unfortunately, one look at my phone tells me I won't have
the luxury of processing anything in peace. I have a missed
call from Blythe, and as much as I'd like to ignore her, I'd
rather get this over with because I'm sure I know what this is
about. At least this will be an easy call. She's heard about the
deal with Pink, surely. The reallocation of charitable funds
that she won't have a say in. Ones she won't be able to
manipulate. And she's calling to scheme and try to talk me
out of it. Well, fuck her. She won't be screwing up this deal,
my company, or my life with her bullshit.

I punch her contact information and let the phone ring.
She answers almost immediately, her voice its usual purr. I
used to find it sexy, but those days are long gone.

"Well, hello, Harrison," she murmurs into the phone. "I'm
surprised you had the time to call me back."

"What do you want, Blythe?" I ask. I'm not interested in
her games.

She giggles. It sounds terrible and has nothing to do with
the connection. She's not a giggler; neither her voice nor her
disposition lends itself to giggling.

"Did I interrupt something?"

"Stop wasting my time," I snap. "I have things to do.
What do you want?"

I can imagine her at home, pacing in her kitchen, or maybe
lounging on the furniture expertly picked by a designer. A

home I'm paying for. Furniture I've paid for. Because everything always goes to her.

But not this time.

"I know, Harrison," she says, a bit of a singsong added to her tone. One that suits her even less than a giggle. "I know what you've been up to."

"I don't care if you know," I say. "I'm committed to this deal and neither you nor your boyfriend will be able to shove a single shady clause into it."

For a moment, there's silence on the other end. That singsong tone catching up with me a moment too late.

"Oh, this isn't about your ridiculous deal," she says. "Though, I must say. I commend you for thinking of it. I told Robert it was petty to try to challenge you for that deal. But no, Harrison. I don't care about that."

"Then what is this about, Blythe?" I say, moments from losing my patience.

"I know about *her*," she says, dragging out the last syllable. The words freeze me as I realize who she's talking about. Emery. But it must be a bluff. How would she know? It's impossible. Unless Claire told her. Which isn't impossible.

"Indeed," Blythe says, and I can hear the cruel smile in her voice even without seeing it. "I know that you've got yourself a *young* little plaything. An intern and a mistress in one package deal. And you know what else I know?"

I don't answer her. I won't give her the satisfaction.

"I know it's time to sign the papers, Harrison," she says. "Or I promise you, you'll regret it."

CHAPTER TWENTY-EIGHT

BEFORE WE LAND, Emery reappears, her hair slightly mussed from sleep. She looks at me shyly as she sinks into the seat next to mine. I know she didn't hear my conversation with Blythe, but something's wrong. I can see it right away. Before I can ask, she speaks.

"Can I ask a favor?" Emery asks. "I know you're going straight from the airport to the office, but I think all of this travel...it's sort of messed with my system. Do you mind if I take a few hours off? I just want to stop at my place and recoup a bit."

Of course it's taken a toll. I've forced the girl to fly back and forth across the country in a matter of days. Even on a private plane, that's not an easy task.

Not to mention I haven't given her much opportunity to sleep.

I nod. "Take the entire day. You were supposed to be out, anyway, since we're back early. Ramon is already working on the Pink deal and Sandy can help me wrap everything up."

She smiles. "Thanks."

I run a finger along her jaw. "Is there anything else?"

She shakes her head. "No."

But I can tell there's something else bothering her. Not that I'm owed an explanation. Going back to the office means going back to reality. And even if this trip has made each of us realize there's something more going on between us…well, I can understand why she might be having second thoughts. God, we're not even a public couple, are we? Blythe's words referring to Emery as my mistress hang over my head. What must this feel like for Emery? Her first sexual partner and she's…

She's my mistress.

For once Blythe is right. It's time to end this divorce nonsense. It's all bullshit. Because the only one who matters to me is Emery. And even if I'd never met Emery, Blythe and I are over. We were over before Emery sailed in the door and dumped coffee all over me. Hell, we were over before Emery even moved to New York.

Fucking with Blythe by dragging this divorce out…it's not worth it anymore. Emery means more to me than exacting any kind of retribution on Blythe. And I can't move forward with Emery with Blythe hanging over us.

I should explain all of this to Emery. But old habits die hard and so instead of pouring my guts out to her I tap my fingers on the armrest and think about it. Besides, actions speak louder than words and I need to back up my words with a signature, one ending my marriage in the only way it still exists—legally.

"You can tell me," I say, instead. "We still have a few hours to go, and I'd like to listen."

She smiles again, her eyes sad. "It's complicated." She shrugs, her eyes shifting away with the movement. "Like inexcusably complicated."

"I think you mean unexplainably complicated." I smile, reminding myself how much more dramatic life felt when I was her age. When every problem felt bigger than it was. "Try me."

"It's not really," she pauses. "I don't think you'd be able to understand."

I frown at her cryptic response. She turns back to the window, watching the clouds streak past us. Is she feeling awkward about us? About the private plane? About the trip in general? About the gifts I've given her, the payments for her student loans and the donation to the charity?

Or you know, my wife?

"I'm not sure New York is going to work out for me," she says, her voice so quiet that I nearly have to lean forward to hear her."

The confession startles me. "Why?"

She sighs. "It's an expensive, complicated city. And nothing is ever quite what it looks like at first glance."

I shake my head, reaching out to take her hand. "So let me help. You'll get a raise when your internship ends. When you're a permanent employee at Duke Capital."

She lets out a sad laugh and pulls back her hand. And now I really don't understand. What the fuck happened between when we boarded this plane and now?

"You can't always be there to rescue me," she says. "I've got to take care of myself."

She blinks her long lashes at me as she looks back, meeting my eyes with hers.

"And besides," she adds. "You're married, remember?"

It's those words that tell me, definitively, that my gut was right. It's time. It's time to finalize the divorce with Blythe, whatever the cost. Whatever it takes to free me to be with Emery, in every sense of the word, then I'll do it. I have to. I'll do whatever it takes to be with her. However she'll have me.

"I won't be for long," I tell her. "I'm going to sign the papers."

She tilts her head. "You are? But why?"

Because of you, I want to say. Because I can't bear the thought of pushing her even further away. I know why she's doing this. She doesn't want to be a mistress, and I've forced her into being one. I need to tread lightly. I don't want to make Emery feel worse. This is all on me, not her.

Claire was right. I've defiled this girl in every sense of the word.

"I should've done it a long time ago," I finally say. "I told you that I was sick of Blythe taking so much from me. Her affair...it was with Robert, my best friend. I told you that. You can't imagine what it feels like, to watch not one but two people you thought cared about you just chuck you out like garbage. I became too fixated on vengeance. It was petty, trying to find a way to make her pay. To keep her from getting anything more from me. And so I dragged it out, for absolutely no legitimate reason."

I let out a bitter laugh. "And now here I am. Screwing myself. Allowing her to hurt me because she's taking you away, inadvertently."

Emery glances away. I worry she'll start to cry again, but then she turns to me and shakes her head.

"No," she says. "She's not."

She leaves her chair and straddles mine, kissing me hungrily and feverishly as I bury my hand in her hair. I kiss her back with the same conviction, hoping that she understands that this is exactly where I want—and possibly need—to be. With her, with everything she is. I kiss every inch of her I can reach, from her nose to her cheeks to her jaw, raining kisses down until I get to her neck and chest. I tell her with every kiss that I'll do anything, be anything that she wants, as long as she stays here with me.

We're alone in the cabin, but I'm not putting on a show for the crew, so I stand, tugging Emery behind me, hand tucked in mine as I walk us back to the bedroom. The sheets are still mussed from her earlier nap, and I drop her gently on top of them. She looks up at me with those big eyes, full of desire and want.

"Take it all off," she demands, gesturing at my clothes. "I want to see all of you."

Her words spark a different idea in me. "What if you're not allowed to?"

She raises an eyebrow. "What do you mean?"

I remove my tie and drop down next to her on the bed, dangling it in front of her. "What if you're not allowed to see me?"

She bites her lip and looks from the tie to me.

"You mean...I'd be blindfolded?"

I nod. "It's something we haven't tried yet. And I do enjoy surprising you."

The lust spikes in her eyes, and I'd love to know what's running through her mind. I imagine she's picturing all the things I've done to her already, and wondering what it would be like if she wasn't able to see my every move. Each touch would be a mystery, a tease.

She nods, more hunger in her eyes. "Let's do it, Mr. Duke," she adds with a bit of cheek.

I'm smiling when I wrap the tie around her head, covering her eyes and tying it in the back. She sits expectantly on the bed, and I consider the best way to begin paying her back in pleasure.

Well, she did want me to take off my clothes.

I remove my shirt and unbuckle my pants, making sure the noise is audible. She licks her lips in response, and her chest rises with a quick intake of breath. My cock twitches as I watch her tongue slide out to wet her lips. Soon, that marvelous tongue will be on me and my cock, but for now, I've promised her new sensations to make her toes curl.

I shrug off my pants and boxer briefs, letting my cock spring free. As if she knows, Emery kneels forward on the bed, reaching for me. I push her hand away and force her to sit back on her knees.

"Am I going to have to tie up your hands, too?" I ask.

She growls in response, and I smirk. Maybe all this defiling isn't such a bad thing.

I slip onto the bed and sit behind her, getting so close that my dick is pressed against her back, hard and ready. She gasps at the feel of it, and then I reach around and massage both of her breasts with my hands as I nip at her neck.

"Harrison," she purrs. "Oh—"

My fingertips flick her nipples, hard and aching beneath my touch. I'd love to flip her over and suck on them, but I wait. There will be time for that.

Instead, I trace my one hand down her stomach, reaching between her legs to tease the lips of her wet pussy. She widens her legs a bit, allowing me more room, and I continue to trace the folds with my fingers.

"More," she gasps. "Please."

"You'll take what you get," I tell her, and she groans as I find her clit and circle it teasingly with my finger.

"I will if you make me," she snaps back, and all the blood remaining in my body rushes to my cock at those words.

If I make her? Well, I can certainly do that.

I remove my fingers and suck on them, letting her hear the pop as I remove them from my mouth. Then I drag the tips of two wet fingers down her torso, slow enough that her breathing increases with anticipation and perhaps a bit of the unknown, before I slide two long fingers into her wet, clenching pussy as she moans and writhes. I keep the other hand tweaking her nipple as I kiss on the back of her neck, relishing her shivers and the way she arches against me.

God, I've got to have her. I can't wait any longer.

"Please," she demands, clearly on the same wavelength, clearly full of the same desire that's coursing through me. "Fuck me," she adds in a bit of a whine, just in case her demand wasn't clear. I snap off the blindfold and she turns, pressing the hot, wet flesh of her pussy against the outline of my cock. God, she's so ready, so impossibly ready.

"Patience," I tease, reaching for my pants on the floor to grab a condom. As I do, she drops her head and gives one long lick to my cock, forcing a low groan out of me that's primal and feral.

"I want you," she demands again. "And I'm taking what I want."

She licks again, from the base to the tip, and then she takes me into her mouth, wet and hot and perfect. My hips jolt forward against her lips, but she puts a hand on my thigh, pressing me back into the bed as her head bobs up and down, taking me deeper than I'd thought she was able.

I could come right now, explode into her mouth, but that's not what I want. I ease her back, and she looks up at me with lust, her lips slick from my dick.

"Who knew you were so naughty?" I ask.

She smiles. "I learned from the best."

Her words alone could tear me apart, but it's her eyes and the way she's looking at me, knowing that I have made her this way. Yet, even with her inexperience, she's also made me. Brought me to the brink of things I never thought possible. And here, with her now, I only want more, more, more.

Because looking at her, with her messy hair and her fresh face, it all hits harder than I expected. I do want to be with her. I want her like this, every day. I want her easy laugh. I want her passion. I want it all.

I slide the condom on over my cock as she wipes her mouth, and then I sit back, kneeling on the bed. She lays down, her legs already falling open, but I shake my head.

"No," I say. "We're trying something new."

I guide her to straddle me so that her pussy is flush against my cock, and she grinds gently against me before I help her into the right position that she can sit down and envelop me while on top of me. Once she understands, she lowers slowly, letting my cock drive up deep inside her waiting pussy.

"Oh—"

Immediately, I notice the change in the sensation. This position pushes me so much deeper inside of her, and as she leans forward, she realizes that it also allows me to rock against her clit. Her jaw drops on a gasp, her face contorting with pleasure as she moves forward, and I wrap one hand around her ass, guiding her motions until she gets the hang of it herself. I use the other to cup the back of her neck, keeping her steady as she writhes on top of me, her breasts bouncing. Her hair's come completely undone, wild around her head, and she's wild, too, lost in the pleasure that we're getting from each other.

Her orgasm shakes through both of us as she grinds forward, and mine comes almost immediately after, exploding inside of her as I watch her lose herself in the throes of our passion. In moments, she collapses on me, still rocking slightly as I remain inside of her.

It's terrifying, the want that slides through me, even now. It's insatiable, something that cannot and will not be fucked away. Whatever it is must be more, and I don't know if that's even what she wants from me.

She touches my face and I open my eyes to find her peering at me.

It doesn't matter what she wants. Whatever it is, I'll give it to her. I'll move heaven and earth to give her what she needs. Because she's changed me, and even if it was possible to go back to who I was before, I don't want to.

CHAPTER TWENTY-NINE

ONCE WE'VE LANDED, Leo picks us up and drops Emery off at her place before taking me directly to the office. With all of the flying, I barely have any concept of time, but it's just past ten in the morning by the time Leo pulls up to Duke Capital. Thank God for the shower on the plane. That and the spring that Emery puts in my step is what is driving me forward.

She fell asleep again after we finished, and I held her until the plane began its descent. She looked so perfect, like she was made to be curled up in my bed, in my arms. And maybe it's selfish, wanting her to stay with me, but I'll do whatever it takes to make it up to her. I'll give her whatever she needs.

It probably is selfish, wanting her to stay with me.

She's young. She probably wants to date a bunch of douchebags before settling into a more serious relationship. With an older, still technically married douchebag.

What troubles me, though, is that, when we dropped her off, some of her sadness from earlier seemed like it was back. I tell myself it's just being back home, the glow of the trip wearing off, and nothing else. Maybe it's knowing that Claire knows. Maybe she feels ashamed or embarrassed. But I'll hold my end of the bargain. I'll keep it professional. Anything

Emery gets will be hard fought, just like she is. If any of them, including Claire, had seen her in that meeting with Monica, they'd understand. She isn't using me as a stepping stone. She isn't getting ahead by being with me.

She's not like that.

She's nothing like Blythe.

And besides, she doesn't need me for anything. She's a talented young woman. Any company in New York would be lucky to have her.

I arrive at the office in a haze of racing thoughts, and it takes Sandy saying my name a few times to make me realize that I've walked through the lobby, taken the elevator to the executive floor, and walked the hall to my office without realizing it. I shake my head and see that she's smiling at me.

"Welcome back, Mr. Duke," she beams in greeting. "Everything is on schedule," she adds. "The conference room is booked for noon so each team can update you on where they're at with their part of the Pink deal."

"Excellent," I say. "Where's Ramon?"

"In his office," she says. "I think he's trying to talk Blythe —erm, Mrs. Lawrence-Duke—into reason. She was ah"— Sandy pauses, attempting to be delicate—"a bit out of sorts at being left out of the loop on the reallocation of charity funds."

I wince. I don't want to see that witch, but I also know it's unavoidable. But the mention of her name has reminded me of something I need to do. I told Emery that I was going to finalize the divorce. And the only way to show her I'm serious, that she's not being strung along, is to follow through.

So, fuck it. I'll sign the papers now. Bickering over negotiations be damned. Then, there won't be anything to hold us back.

"Excuse me, Sandy," I say. "I forgot to do something."

She nods, looking slightly confused but understanding. "Of course, Mr. Duke."

I turn and head back for the elevator, zipping down to

Claire's floor without ever even setting down my briefcase. I find her assistant looking surprised at my unannounced walk in, but I cut her off before she can say anything.

"I believe Claire left some papers for me to sign," I tell her. "My divorce papers. I need them now."

She blinks at me, clearly caught off guard and unsure how to respond without Claire here, but she seems to recall she ultimately works for me and snaps to attention. She excuses herself and heads into Claire's office, and when she returns, she holds out a manila envelope, sealed with my name on it. There's also a sticky note that reads, "For whenever he's finally ready." Something tells me the assistant was supposed to remove that, but I don't care. I thank the girl and leave, relief practically rolling off of me in waves. I've never been so ready to end something in my life.

To begin something else.

Once I'm back up in my office, I make quick work of the papers. A few slices of my pen and the work's done, signed and ready. Already, it feels like a weight's fallen off of me. Now I can focus on the future. Or at the very least, today.

Sandy was right about everyone working efficiently to close this deal. When I find Ramon in his office—thankfully alone and without Blythe in sight—he fills me in on everything, bringing me up to speed on what everyone is doing to make this pitch to Pink a reality.

"Impressive idea, Harrison," he says, and the admiration is genuine. "We're solving multiple issues at once with this one. How did you come up with this?"

I shrug, trying not to reveal too much and overplay my hand.

"You were right," I say. "Emery was an asset on the trip. She was able to charm Monica enough to listen, and then the idea came to me. I knew we had to find a way to right the wrongs from the charity, and this is just a start."

Ramon nods in approval. "Well, we'll still need to figure out what to do moving forward. You and I both know that there are more issues with Blythe's department than just this job. Also...something was off with Blythe today, Harrison. I couldn't put my finger on it. She wasn't happy about the deal, but she also didn't fight it. Not like she usually does."

I sigh. He might as well know. "She was pressuring me on the divorce earlier, and I think she's probably just smug that she's about to win."

Except really, she isn't. I see that now. I'm the one securing a win by being free of her.

"Really?" Ramon asks, his eyebrows shooting up. "Well, congratulations, man. I know that wasn't easy."

"At some point," I say, "you just have to start living your life again. Staying married to her was only hurting me, and I finally realized that."

"Gee," Ramon says, rolling his eyes. "If only someone had told you that."

I chuckle, glancing back at the pictures Ramon has decorating his office. There are so many of his family, of his kids climbing on his back, of he and his wife at their wedding. The love in their eyes is so potent, I almost have to look away.

And then it hits me.

Love.

"Oh fuck," I say.

"What?" Ramon asks. "Something wrong with the deal?"

"No," I say, slowly, as the details come back to me.

Emery in my arms. Emery looking at me from across the room. Her laugh, cutting through the noise of my life.

The divorce papers might have granted me freedom, but they aren't enough. They won't erase the tiny apartment that Emery lives in, and they won't bring our two worlds together. They won't keep Emery here with me, by my side. And they won't smother the ache in my heart when I think about her.

Not now. Not when I've finally pulled my head out of my ass, my reality being crystal clear.

I'm in love with her.

CHAPTER THIRTY

LOVE. It's a word that I thought had slipped out of my vocabulary. Permanently. I was not the kind of guy who would have a photograph of my wife in my office. Never again. No photographs of kids or family vacations. A crayon drawing smudged with grape jelly would be as out of place in my office as a cheap suit. I would be a bachelor, someone who would occasionally find a woman to spend the hours of a cold night with. But love? Love was never going to enter the equation. Love was no longer for a realist like me. It was for fools, quite honestly.

And I'm the biggest fool of all because I know better and I don't care.

It's her, of course. Emery. It's everything she is and everything she stands for. It's the feeling in my chest when I think of her. The smile it brings to my face when I recall the day she plowed into me with coffee. The tug on my heart when I think of the way she looked at me when she swung open her apartment door that night I picked her up for the charity event. It's the way her eyes light up at simple joys, like cheap food, or selecting some silly movie on demand while lounging on my sofa. It's how complete I feel with her beside me. It's how she's not afraid to tell me what she thinks. It's her honesty, her pureness through to her soul.

She's the one.

Sure, I'm finding her a bit later in my life, and a bit earlier in hers. But she's the one.

Is it quick? Sure. But it doesn't matter. I spent years thinking I was in love with Blythe, but it was an illusion. Or perhaps it was real at one time, and grew into manipulation and greed. I don't know, and I don't really care. Not anymore. Because I'm grateful now for the past. It makes me appreciate Emery all the more. I don't know if I'd so easily recognize what I have with Emery now if I didn't have anything to compare it to, if I didn't have the dark to compare to the light. If I didn't have lies to compare with truth.

The noon meeting is intolerable. Which just goes to show the level of my distraction. I should be reveling in watching the deal come together. In watching the team I've built effectively do their parts to make it all happen.

Yet all I can think about is my next step.

When the meeting ends I tell Sandy I'm cutting out early for the day. She nods, as if it's normal for me to leave work fifteen minutes early, let alone a couple of hours. "Enjoy your evening, Mr. Duke," she tells me. "You deserve it."

Once in the car, I direct Leo to take me to a high-end jewelry store. One of the best in New York, and thus the world really.

"Needing a special gift, sir?" His smile from the front seat is smug. I'm tempted to tell the old goat to mind his business but fuck it, I'm a fool in love, so I let it slide with a noncommittal shrug. All I can think about is Emery and what she'll think of what I have in mind. Because what I have in mind is a bit more than a special gift and more of a lifelong commitment.

The jeweler works quickly, eager to help me find the perfect combination of a diamond and band that Emery will love. One that is worthy of her joy and innocence and heart-stopping charm. A ring fit for a forever romance.

An oval diamond, large, surrounded by a halo of rosy pink diamonds set in a platinum and diamond band.

It's romantic and classic and timeless. Like Emery.

My phone buzzes occasionally with some work-related issue or other, but I ignore it. My focus is here, pacing in a jewelry store waiting for the diamond to be set into the band so that I can leave with it today. So that I can give it to Emery.

Today.

Because I don't think I can wait. Not now that I've finally come to my senses. Not when I can ease the doubts I know she was having. About us. About what kind of future I represented. About her place in my life, and her title in it. She's not a mistress. God, no. Perhaps we're skipping the girlfriend step. But I know what I want. This, I'm sure, will show her that I'm serious and that what we have is real and good and honest. She'll know that I'm not just some asshole showering her with temporary gifts or bullshit. I'm the man who wants to stand beside her always, caring for her the way she deserves to be cared for.

Forever.

I don't want her to leave New York. And I sure as hell don't want her to leave me.

Once the ring is finished, the jeweler hands it over in a velvet box. I've held one of these before. Many times. Many velvet boxes with no end of high-end trinkets. None have felt like this. Like I'm giving a piece of myself with the gift. I feel it when I place it in my pocket. This ring is meant to belong to Emery, just as we're meant to belong to each other.

Leo drives me to Emery's neighborhood, and I laugh at myself a bit as we pull up. I should have a plan, a better plan than sprinting up her steps and asking her to marry me. Something more romantic, or at the very least, more elaborate. A dinner, a rented-out museum, a Grammy winner belting out a love song as I drop to one knee. But fuck it. I'm eager and an eager man is not a romantic one.

Leo stops at the curb outside Emery's building and if possible, it seems even shabbier than when I was last here, but I'm sure it's my imagination. I exit the car and button my suit jacket, taking a breath.

This is it. And I've never been so sure of anything in all of my life.

I take the steps two at a time until I'm at her apartment. Inside, I hear commotion. Her roommates, no doubt. There's raucous laughter, and it takes me several knocks before someone answers. It's a girl with long, curly hair and a distinctly thrift-store look, but when I tell her I'm here for Emery she perks up.

"Come on in, suit," she says. "She's in her room."

I thank her and walk inside. Once I'm there, I see that the laughter was due to the TV. Four people are crowded onto the couch across from it, pointing and shrieking at the characters. I inch past them, none of them even glancing my way.

Emery's door flies open when I knock. She looks annoyed until she sees me standing there, and then her mouth falls open.

"Harrison," she says. "What are you doing here?"

She's in jeans and an old T-shirt, and yet, she's never looked more beautiful. Her hair's pulled back in a ponytail, exactly the same style it was in the first day we met, and her lips are pouty and her eyes are bright. I pull her to me in a kiss, and she responds eagerly, our tongues exploring each other in movements that are both new and already perfectly familiar.

This, I think. *This.* I could kiss her until the end of time and never get tired of it.

Eventually, she pulls back, smiling.

"Well, this is a great surprise," she says. "Is the deal done?"

"Yes," I say, "but that's not why I needed to see you."

She opens the door wider so that I can step inside. Her room's small, which I expected. It's lived in, with pictures hung up by clips around a mirror propped over her dresser and clothes hanging on a rack in lieu of an actual closet. There's a quilt on her bed that's clearly handmade, squares of turquoise and pink sewn together by hand.

Emery follows my gaze. "My grandma made that for me."

I smile. "It's you."

I continue to look around her room. A small bookshelf with some well-loved paperbacks. A desk full of papers, many of them printed copies of materials I sent her for the conference. She's added notes and annotations in brightly colored pens.

All of it's so light and fresh, just like her.

"Harrison," she says, nudging me with her arm. "Not that I'm not happy to see you, but what's going on?"

I take a breath. As much as I want to yank the ring out of my pocket and slide it on her finger, I do, in fact, need a better plan than that. No proposal will be worthy of her, but I can do better than dropping to my knee in her bedroom with her roommates just outside the door. I'm not in my twenties, for fuck's sake.

We'll go to dinner tonight. I'll let her pick. Falafel or a fancy steakhouse, or some god-awful touristy restaurant she'll be charmed by. Whatever she wants. Or maybe we'll go back to my place. Privacy. Get something delivered. Or we can go to Paris, if she's up to more flying. Whatever she wants.

But first, I need to clue her in on the direction this is heading. On where I'm at.

"I signed the papers," I tell her. "I'm officially divorced."

For a moment, she just stares at me with her wide eyes. And then, she begins to shake her head before she throws her arms around me.

"Oh my God," she says. "Harrison, I'm so happy for you."

"It's for you," I tell her. "You're the reason. Everything else just didn't matter when I stacked it up against you."

She pulls back from the hug with tears in her eyes. One spills over and I swipe it away with my finger.

"You're my reason, too," she whispers. "I mean, not for getting divorced. But for…for everything else."

I bring her hands to my lips, pressing a kiss to the back of her hand.

"Then we should celebrate," I say. "Dinner. Tonight. What do you say?"

She smiles but bites her lip, glancing at her phone. Does she have plans? She wasn't even supposed to be home today. We were still supposed to be at the conference, so what gives?

Unbidden, doubts creep up. She's hiding something. But I push those thoughts aside. Those thoughts are leftovers, remnants of the horror that Blythe put me through. I won't let them wreck my relationship with Emery.

Emery's eyes slide back to mine and she grins, an easy smile.

"Of course," she says, tucking her phone into her back pocket. "I'd love to. We should celebrate. Just…give me a second to change? Somehow, I don't think this will be okay for whatever restaurant you have in mind."

"It's up to you," I tell her, pressing a kiss to her temple as she shivers against me. "But I certainly wouldn't be opposed to you putting on one of those sexy-as-hell dresses that you look so good in."

She giggles and waves me away. "Impatient man."

"For you?" I say. "Always."

She smiles again and grabs something from the rack that functions as her closet.

"I'll be right back," she says. "Just make yourself comfortable for a bit."

I watch her leave, nearly laughing at her need to leave the

room to change after everything we've done together. But instead, I relish the way her ass looks from behind in those jeans. They hug her in places that cause my mind to wander to visualizing her bent over just so, naked. I'm about to call her back and tell her that she can keep them on no matter where we go.

But then I notice something that makes me stop.

In all of my years with Blythe, one thing I became incredibly accustomed to was her handwriting. It was full of sharp loops, high and imposing, just like her. There's a rushed quality to her signature, like a hint that granting you her signature was an inconvenience for her. Anyone receiving it should be grateful. At least, that's how it always read to me. I'm admittedly biased.

But it's a signature I would recognize anywhere, and it's sticking out of something in a pile of mail on Emery's dresser.

I glance at the door. Emery's footsteps have disappeared and the sound of a door shutting tells me she's closed herself in the bathroom to get ready.

I'm not letting Blythe ruin this relationship, I tell myself. *I'm not going to let Blythe's lies make me think the worst of this girl.*

I sit on the bed, staring at the slip of paper. It's just the end of her signature, on what looks like a check. But whatever it is, it isn't any of my business, and I should need to leave it alone.

Except that I can't.

It doesn't help that in a bedroom the size of Emery's the dresser is all of an arm length's away. I pick up the stack of magazines and bills—many of them stamped "Overdue"—and fish out the paper.

And I was right.

It is a check.

Written from Blythe Lawrence-Duke to Emery Mills.

For $50,000.

And there, sitting beside it, is a note, all of it in the same loops, the same taunting script of the signature that I signed beside earlier.

Emery,

You're a doll. Thanks for solving my Harrison problem.

With endless gratitude,

Blythe

The world might spin. It might just be my reality tilting on its axis. It's impossible to know. All I can see is the letter, those words, and the $50,000 check blaring like a megaphone in my head. I see it all blinking behind my eyelids, even after I've left Emery's bedroom. After I've passed the television-watching roommates and let myself out the front door of her apartment, slipping back into the oblivion that is New York.

The Intern Trilogy continues with The Billionaire's Mistake.

The Billionaire's Mistake is a classic billionaire-chases-former-virgin romance - if your idea of classic is steamy, steamy angst with another plot twist that will make you gasp...

No one says no to me.

I've never worked to get laid in my life.

Women throw themselves at my feet. My last name is enough for models, socialites, actresses, and A-listers--I hardly even have to buy them dinner first.

Emery is nothing like normal women.

She seduced me, gave me her first time, and suddenly I'm the one on my knees.

Finding out that she was keeping secrets from me should

have made my life easier. I could go back to living it on my own terms. No attachments, no obligations. No big blinky eyes begging me for more. When she walked away, I should have thrown a party.

But she doesn't get to just walk away.

I'm the one who says when this is over.

And her perfect, sweet *small town* is an addiction I can't kick.

There's no way I'm letting her get away that easily. It's time to remind her exactly what she's missing. I might even have to remind her twice. Fine, three times, max.

She belongs at my side. In my bed.

And she'd better not be keeping any other secrets from me.

Get The Billionaire's Mistake.

PAIGE PRESS

Paige Press isn't just Laurelin Paige anymore...

Laurelin Paige has expanded her publishing company to bring readers even more hot romances.

Sign up for our newsletter to get the latest news about our releases and receive a free book from one of our amazing authors:

Stella Gray
CD Reiss
Jenna Scott
Raven Jayne
JD Hawkins
Poppy Dunne

ALSO BY LIA HUNT

The Intern Trilogy

The Billionaire's Intern
The Billionaire's Mistake
The Billionaire's Promise

ABOUT THE AUTHOR

Lia Hunt is a pen name for two writers who adore billionaires and virgins with scorching love scenes, jaw-dropping cliffhangers, and swoony happy endings.

Made in United States
North Haven, CT
03 June 2022

19838329R00139